Sherlock H-

THE GHC

"BOOK TWO: THE W

John Pir\.

Mind Control

Harry Syms was the best damned gardener that Buckingham Palace had ever had. He could make a weed blossom into pink and yellow flowers. He could make hand-sized roses as big as the Queen's crown. He just had the knack of it. He talked to his garden, and it listened. He knew it and everyone else knew it. But more importantly, Prince Churchill knew it. His father was too busy with states of affair to notice, but the Prince noticed. He saw the work done by Harry every morning and afternoon out in the plush gardens behind his office. It lightened the ever-increasing pressure of his office, which had become both burdensome and disquieting as rumors and facts about the attempts at using occult weapons and weapons of a science unknown to the Britains grew stronger and were corroborated. Often at the expense of good men and women who acted as spies for His Majesty, King Andrew.

Harry knew that much and appreciated his royal peers more for it. They depended on him to beautiful lives fraught with stress and danger; and he depended on them letting him continue to admonish his gardens to grow and prosper.

As he gathered his tools in the shed, he had to the side of the building, he noticed that one very important one was missing. His pruning shears. He glanced around quickly. Where could he have put those?

A man who resembled himself stood behind him.

He gave the man a stare. "What the...?"

The man put a hand on Harry's forehead and pressed his thumb into the spot where the third eye, the middle of the forehead, would be.

Harry's eyes went wide as tiny moons and then his jaw went slack.

"Do as I say!" The man told Harry.

Harry nodded.

1

The man took his thumb from Harry's forehead and motioned to the floor of the shed. Harry sat down, closed his eyes and the man handed him a knife. "Use it!"

Harry opened his eyes to look at the object placed in his hands. "Not likely!"

"You...will...use...it!" The man insisted.

Harry began to babble like an idiot as his right hand, holding the knife, came closer and closer to his throat. What was going on?

"My hand...I can't control it." He whimpered, tears coming to his eyes. He looked at the man standing over him. "Why?"

The man smiled. "Nothing personal. Really. You're just collateral damage, Harry." The man replied with a heavy German accent.

The man shrugged on clothing that was a duplicate of Harry's, took the pruning shears that Harry had been looking for and walked from the shed. He looked back inside just as Harry, still whimpering and crying, slashed his throat open.

"Now there's a good fellow."

He shut the door of the shed, then said in a low voice, "Heil Himmler!"

He left the shed, twirling the pruner like a toy in his right hand and whistled, "God Save the King." as he went to visit the gardens in the back of the palace.

Behind him something struck the door of the shed hard. Once. Then a trail of blood began oozing from beneath the door onto the dirt surrounding the shed.

Buckingham Palace

Prince Churchill spun on his hills to face Captain Byrnes as he entered his small office down the hall from his father's, King Andrew. "So glad you could make it, Captain." He greeted cheerfully.

Captain Byrant Dodge Byrnes smiled, revealing the gap between his two front teeth, which normally he hid by not smiling. It embarrassed him so. "Likely story. But it'll have to do."

He sat down without being asked to opposite Prince Churchill, who proceeded to pour tea for both from a finely chiseled silver teapot with dragons for handles. "You've heard of course."

"If you mean about Houdini's flat being blown up." He nodded. "Most certainly." He leaned forward, his eyes bright with intelligence and concern. "But if you expect me to believe that a dragon caused the damage..."

Prince Churchill sat down and offered the Captain a teacup, and then took up his own. He took a sip, then his eyes locked onto the Captain's. "How long we known each other, Bernie?"

The Captain stiffened. Prince Churchill never got personal unless he meant to slam you against the wall.

Prince Churchill laughed. "I'm not going to slam you against the wall, Bernie."

The Captain stiffened even more. "You read me too well."

Churchill opened a small humidor to his left and plucked a fat cigar from it. He clipped the tip of it, then bent forward.

Captain Bernie pulled a match from the right upper pocket of his uniform and struck it with a thumb, causing it to burst into life. He held the match to the cigar as Churchill drew on it. It began to glow.

Captain Byrnes flipped the match expertly into the tiny silver cigar tray to the left on the desk that was shaped like a leering mermaid. It slid down her tail into the bowl that accommodated matches and stubbed cigars.

"Never miss a shot." Churchill stated with amusement.

"Or you."

"That's because your thoughts play on your face like a child plays in the backyard. Quite extensively." Prince Churchill replied with a chuckle. He set his teacup down, crossed his arms on his desk, which was made of a fine rosewood and covered with a bright yellow linen. Atop the linen was an inkwell, one of the newer typing machines, one of Edison's teles sat on a thick block base and a writing pad with myriad notes scribbled in all directions. It was his way of organizing his thoughts Though God only knew how anyone, even he could make sense of them, they were so jumbled.

"Very well."

Prince Churchill smiled. It was warm, but behind it was a man of strong determination and a will that dwarfed that of any ordinary politician, or even King. Even the King bowed to Prince Churchill's will; knowing that his son was much stronger willed; and by orders of magnitude, much smarter in the ways of the world...and war, in this case.

The Captain squirmed uneasily a moment, then sighed. "Okay. I get it. So, a dragon...whatever thing...attacked poor Harry's domicile. Destroyed it..."

"And killed about a score of other people besides." Prince Churchill reminded the Captain.

The Captain investigated his teacup. He thought to take a sip but felt the bile rising into his throat would make it bitter. "War is never pretty."

"Then you admit it is war."

The Captain looked up; his eyes narrowed with anger. "Of the lowest character; the vilest nature."

"Is war ever truly civil, Bernie? Men, women, and children always die in them. No one ever dies thanking their murderers, do they?"

Bernie had no reply to that because it was true. No one really wanted to die. It just came and they had to accept it.

Prince Churchill nodded. He stood up and went to look out his window upon the gardens his view provided. "There was a time, I am told, before King Arthur and Excalibur. Before the Druids came and Merlin. A time when magic was not so strong. When it was rumored and a tale of old wives and old folk tales."

He watched a gardener trimming his favorite roses. Harry from the looks since he was the only one allowed in the private area. But the man was taking a long time to do the bush. He frowned. Then shrugged. Harry was a good man; he could be allowed for some discrepancies.

He turned around to face the Captain again. "Bernie, we must face reality. The old rules and ways of life are no longer on the table. This is down and dirty, vile corruption we're dealing with. We can no longer just sit back and wait for the other side to come at us and then repel them like in the last war."

The Captain straightened up. He sipped his tea in one long gulp. He set his cup down. "You're telling me that the Sweinhunds are back at our throats again!"

"No, I'm telling you that they are not."

The Captain started to relax. "Then there's another party in power?"

Prince Churchill didn't answer. He didn't need to. His expression said it all.

The Captain rose to stand beside his friend at the window. "Lovely roses."

"I especially enjoy the violet ones. A mutation I've been told. A blend of the orange and the blue."

"I've never seen a blue rose."

Prince Churchill smiled. "Oh, they're pretty enough, but rare and very difficult to grow in our colder climate. I hear they do quite well in the Americas."

"Prince."

"Church, please."

"Church." The Captain amended. "You don't think the Americans are behind this recent tragedy, do you?"

"Them scoundrels?" He shook his head. "Hardly. Were they that low and vile, Mark Twain would have abandoned the colonies and moved here at once!"

The Captain's eyes noted the gardener fumbling in a large kit at his feet.

"I see. Then it is the Germans only."

"Yes. We believe so."

"The Verboten party we've been hearing so many rumors about?"

"Exactly. But they're not rumors. They're real."

"I don't like what I hear of them."

"You shouldn't, Bernie. They're not nice people. They are led by a scoundrel named Herr Himmler."

"I have heard of him. Too much. He suppresses dissent through repression and disparaging of people's virtue."

"He discredits them; then he removes them."

The Prince turned to look at the Captain. "Permanently."

"DOWN!" The Captain yelled, then slammed himself into the Prince knocking them both to the floor behind the desk.

The window is shattered by bursts of machine gun fire.

Bullet holes shattered the far walls of the office, slammed into the door, ripping it apart, sending shreds of wood and plaster into the air and into the Captain and the Prince's bodies. Glass flew everywhere.

Then nothing.

The Captain doesn't wait. He leaped off the Prince, then out the window.

The Gardener ran for the far wall of the garden, tossing his machine gun to the ground as he leapt and vanished over it before the Captain can draw his own weapon to fire.

He heard gunfire on the other side of the wall. By the time he reached it he saw Royal Guards closing in on a fallen man, sprawled across the drive-in front. Blood began to pool about his body. It's the gardener.

The Captain leapt over the fence, and then worked his way to the fallen man the same time as the cautious Royal Guards surrounded the fallen man. He touched the man's neck and shook his head.

The Royal Guards suddenly stiffened.

"Your Majesty." The Captain greeted without looking.

Prince Churchill moved past him and gently rolled over the body of the gardener. "This is good. I was quite worried for a moment there that I had lost a good man."

The Captain gave him a surprised look. "How can an assassination attempt be good?"

"For one." The Prince said in a pleasant voice. "I am still alive." He laughed. "Two. You are as well, thanks to your quick thinking. And three, he's not my real gardener, Harry Syms. I would have hated to lose such a good man. My gardens would never be the same."

The Captain barked with laughter.

A Royal Guard rushed forward from the side of the building. "Your Majesty!"

"What's the emergency? Everything's under control." Prince Churchill demanded.

"The Gardener. Harry." The Royal Guard stammered. He had been quite close to the man. Even inviting him over to share dinner with his wife and young son. He couldn't look the Prince in the eyes. His heart felt so bad he wanted to tear it out of his chest.

"Out with it!" The Prince demanded, his own heart starting to pound with what he feared he would hear.

The Royal Guard looked up into the Prince's eyes.

"NO!" Prince Churchill shouted.

The Captain wanted to give his friend a hug to console him as the Prince stood there frozen like a statue, except for his eyes, which began to swell up with tears. He lifted his eyes and focused on Captain Byrant, who had stood there watching his friend's anger and grief. Both men were agreed one thing for sure.

"This is not the end of it!" Prince Churchill swore.

Threads

Captain Byrnes strode towards his command car, where his best friend and currently chauffeur waited behind the wheel. His thoughts were everywhere but upon business this morning. He looked back over his shoulder at the entrance to Buckingham Palace and the Guards standing there as stiff as statues, then back at the command car.

What he had been told had not only surprised him but had turned his entire philosophic view of reality upside down and inside out. What he had seen in the shed and in the Prince's office; that had turned his world into shades of red. Anger at himself for not being able to stop the assassination attempt in the first place; anger at his friend having to lose a man in such a horrible way. He still couldn't understand why the man had cut his own throat open. Why would he have done that? He had no history to indicate he was suicidal.

He cursed silently. War was hell. But this new war. It was far worse. Weapons that were devised of curses. Crystal balls that could investigate your very thoughts and most private rooms. Wickedly divisive and horribly offensive to his British way of thinking.

It just wasn't gentlemanly to do either. Cursing he could understand. Damn you all. And bollocks to hell and back. But a curse that was a weapon that could summon a demon and dispose of whomever the curse was aimed at. That was not only insane, but terribly frightening.

How do you fight invisible enemies? Was that how the gardener had been murdered? By a curse? The thought of it sent shivers up and down his spine and made him feel as if he might choke for a moment.

The Captain climbed into the command car next to his friend, Lieutenant Jollywald, who gave him a sympathetic glance.

"You heard?"

His friend nodded. "The Prince sent a messenger. We heard the shooting out here as well."

"We?"

"Yes, Captain." Holmes greeted from the back seat.

The Captain turned to look.

"I didn't see you."

"I make it a habit of not being seen when I don't want to be." Holmes replied.

He gestured to the man seated next to him with a black medical bag. "This is Watson, of course."

"Of course. You two are inseparable, I understand."

Watson started to comment, but Holmes waved him off. "Captain, this is no accident that you were attacked the same time as we arrived."

The Captain gave him a blank look.

Holmes arched an eyebrow pensively. "You didn't know? Prince Churchill didn't inform you at all, did he?"

"Of what?"

"That you will be working closely with us from now on."

Watson snorted. "So, like the man to keep his own friends in the dark. Enough to bugger one off sometimes."

Holmes gave half a smile. "He might be one of the toughest leaders we've ever had, Watson, don't be so quick to judge him. We are going to need men with wills of iron and nerves of steel with what is coming."

Watson snorted again, unphased by Holmes comment. "Never said I was judging him."

Holmes laughed.

"Captain, if you and Lieutenant Jollywald will be so good as to drive us to Baker Street, we can then have that chat that's been needed since the incident last night and the one at the Palace just this day."

"You two know about the murder and the attempt at the Prince's life as well?" The Captain demanded.

Holmes lost his smile. "When it comes to Harry and Challenger." He paused. "We are always involved. And the Prince sent for us immediately once it was found out that the Gardener was murdered."

"What do you know?"

Sherlock looked away. "We will talk about that. Later."

Aftermath of a Demon

Harry and Challenger examined the building that he and Harry had just managed to escape from.

"Truly a tragic circumstance, Harry. I'm sorry for your loss." Challenger commented, his voice sounding as strained as his figure was. His clothing was burnt in places, torn, and soiled from the tumble they had both taken in the street after the explosion.

Harry, not feeling or looking much better, waved a crisped wand, that looked more like a burnt matchstick than a wand capable of magic, shook his head. "It took me a decade to build up the magical stores I've lost."

"Rather think this was an accident of magic than intent of purpose." Challenger responded, and then shook his head. "Not bloody likely though, is it?"

"No. We both saw the same thing."

"It's war then." Challenger said.

"War." Harry agreed.

Holmes and Watson came to stand beside the two.

"Sorry, Harry." Watson said. "If you need a place to stay for a time, we have an extra room we can let you have."

Holmes gave Watson a look. "The study?"

Watson glared at Holmes. "You have a problem with that?"

"Not at all. I was of a mind to say the same but feared you might find it too bothersome."

Watson snorted. "Friends are everything."

Challenger gave Watson a friendly smile. "Well, most friends anyway."

Challenger's smile vanished.

Holmes shook his head. "Then we are one mind in this. Harry?"

Harry looked into his palms as if they would reveal something; then he looked up, tears in his eyes. "I don't know what to say."

Challenger nudged him in the ribs. "Say yes, mighty magician man!"

Harry gave Challenger a scowl. "No wonder Watson said what he just did."

Challenger broke into laughter.

They all did.

Scar

Commandant Kepfler towered over Scar, who himself, towered over all the soldiers of the hidden chamber. The only person who truly frightened him was the giant before him. Not because of his size; but because of his mystery. There was too much about this man, this giant, that he did not understand.

And that frightened him. Greatly.

Commandant Kepfler stabbed Scar in the chest with his meaty right index finger. "This was supposed to be a clean kill."

"Herr Beimler was a sadist." Scar retorted angrily. "Your man. Not mine! You want perfection; give me men I can trust to do what they are told to do."

Commandant Kepfler swept his iron fist out and clasped Scar by his throat. He lifted him effortlessly into the air until his feet were dangling.

Everyone in the chamber froze. Fearing the worst, they waited.

"You dare accuse me of failure?"

Scar stared into the Commandant's eyes. "You dare to accuse me of yours?"

Commandant Kepfler suddenly became aware that everyone was watching him. Some were even putting hands on their weapons. He growled like a beast for a moment, then dropped Scar.

Scar stumbled a moment, but quickly regained his feet. He rubbed at his throat. "I fear no man. Or whatever you are!"

Commandant Kepfler gave Scar a nasty scowl. "There are far worse than I to fear, Scar. Far worse. And far worse things."

Scar stepped closer to the giant and stabbed him in the chest with his own forefinger. "Whose damned war is this, Commandant Kepfler? Yours and your foul companions? Or Herr Himmler's?"

Again, Commandant Kepfler eyed the still silent men gathered about the room. He sat back down. "We will talk about this later when we both have cooler heads."

Scar pushed his advantage. "No. We will talk about it now."

Commandant Kepfler gave Scar a look of pure hatred. "You dare to speak to me like that!"

Scar laughed.

Commandant Kepfler swung his arm out so fast Scar had no chance whatsoever to dodge. He was swept up into the air and flung a dozen feet to slam against a desk, which overturned, taking with it a man on a typewriter and several chairs.

Scar laid there stunned.

The Commandant stood up. He glared at all the angry faces now watching him.

"I am the one running this. Not this man. If you have a problem with that, speak up now."

No one moved. The room became suddenly busy.

221B

Harry and Watson sat silently near the fire. Harry wore slippers and a gaudy velvet red gown with yellow flowers on it. Watson did his best not to laugh but couldn't help it. Harry glared at him. Watson stopped, then began laughing again.

"What's so damned funny, Watson?"

Watson wiped at the crumbs on his mustache, then set his coffee cup down and away from him at the table he was near. "I never imagined I could be rooming with two such eccentric fellows at the same time. What blessed luck I have?"

"I could say the same, John." Ms. Hudson said, having heard the conversation as she entered. "Being as I've had to put up with two now for a few years."

"Point taken." Watson contritely answered.

Harry slapped Watson on his right knee. "Cheer up, old man. This won't be longer than a year or two."

Watson gave Harry a look of utter horror.

Harry barked with laughter.

"What are you two fighting about now?" Holmes demanded as he came into the sitting room and sat at the dining table, where a spread of fresh sandwiches and scones lay on a large silver platter, with several white napkins and silverware spread before them. He took a napkin, spread it neatly across his lap, and then a small China plate, placed a sandwich on it, then a knife and fork and began slicing the sandwich into quarter sections.

"Why ever in the world do you do that, Holmes?" Harry asked. "It's already bite size."

Holmes ignored him and put the first slice into his mouth to eat.

Watson slapped Harry on his right knee. "Cheer up, old man. You'll only have to put up with us for another year or two."

Harry gave Watson a look of horror, which quickly broke into a series of grins. He barked with laughter, reached for a sandwich, and popped it into his mouth. Thus, shutting himself up.

Ms. Hudson smiled at the men, then said to Watson, "I'm going to the market for some fresh produce. Would you like to accompany me, John?"

Watson jumped up. "I would indeed, Ms. Hudson. I would indeed."

Harry jumped up. "I could help."

"I need to speak with you, Harry." Holmes interrupted.

Harry gave him a disappointed look, then Ms. Hudson and Watson as they exited the room and went downstairs.

"He has all the fun."

"How is Mina doing these days?" Holmes asked. Which totally surprised Harry, as that was the last thing, he would've thought Holmes to ask him about.

"Uh. All right. I guess."

Holmes took another slice of sandwich and nibbled at it on the end of his fork, and then eyed Harry sternly. "When are you going to admit you still have feelings for this woman?"

"My God! Holmes! She's not a woman!"

Holmes set his fork down on his plate and wiped his hands on his napkin. "I see. And she has no feelings for you either?"

"Why are you making this so complicated?"

Holmes gave Harry a long look. "I once loved a woman."

Harry shut up what he was about to say. Holmes rarely talked about the past.

"She was elegant, smart and beautiful beyond measure." Holmes explained, his eyes growing distant as he remembered her. "She was strong. Stronger than any I had ever met before."

"What happened to her?"

Holmes focused on Harry. "She died."

"Oh."

"Tragically."

"I'm sorry, Holmes."

"In my arms."

Harry averted his eyes to his lap, suddenly ashamed of his own feelings or lack of them. "I can't help what I feel. I don't love her anymore."

"Did you ever?"

Harry looked Holmes in the eyes to lie to him but couldn't.

"I see." Holmes said softly.

He rose, placed his napkin on his plate, folding it neatly, and then headed for his room. He stopped to look back at Harry. "Love is sometimes like a furious storm, sweeping you from one direction to the next; sometimes it is like the gentle spring rains; but it is always something that every heart cherishes when it is gone. For a long time." Holmes told Harry and then stepped into his room.

Harry sat there, perplexed, confused, and angry. Perplexed as to why Holmes chose this moment to dredge up the past. Confused about what he was feeling now. And angry that he was feeling anything at all.

"Damn you, Sherlock!" He cursed.

"But why?" Mina asked she stepped into the room, noticeably without Ms. Hudson or Watson following her.

Harry stood up immediately, his heart pounding. "I wasn't angry at him."

Mina gave him a knowing smile.

"All right, blast it all! I was mad, am, mad at him." Flabbergasted at his outrageous display of emotions, he threw himself down on his chair, folded his arms and began to pout like a small child.

Mina laughed. "Always the Harry I knew."

"Am not!" He said in an almost childlike voice.

Her face lost its smile and her eyes some of the glitter he first saw. That brought him out of himself long enough to force him to rise and go to her. He took one of her hands and kissed it lightly. "I am glad to see you again."

She noticed that his kiss lingered a bit longer than was proper for such; but she said nothing.

He let go and looked into her eyes. "You heard what happened?"

"Oh, Ms. Hudson and I talk a bit."

Harry blushed. "That's what I was afraid of. Snitch!"

She laughed, color coming back into her face again as her more bubbly side surfaced.

"Harry, when are we going to stop playing these foolish games and admit that we have been playing foolish games with each other?"

"Probably never." He said, and she said at the same time.

That made Harry laugh. "You read me all too well, Miss Harker."

"And you...not I so much."

He sighed. He took her hand again and sat her down next to the fire beside him at the other chair. "I'm so confused. So much has happened since..."

"Since..." She nodded. "Always since!" She exclaimed. "Since."

She looked into his eyes. "Harry, I know it's not appropriate, but I won't have you live like this. Father won't have you live like this."

Harry shook his head. "Tell the Count I appreciate his offer." He smiled into her eyes. "More than likely your offer, since the old bat hates me with every inch of his body."

"Such as it is." Mina joked.

"Yes. That too." He looked away a moment. "It's in some ways like I got a clean slate; a fresh start."

"How so?" She asked, a look of concern touching her eyes.

He saw it. "Don't worry. I'm not going to do anything rash."

"It seems like you don't have to these days. What with all these monsters popping up willy nilly all over London."

"Yes. There's that too. Actually, that's pretty much describes it in a nutshell."

"So, what do you intend to do? You can't live here forever."

"Nor would I want to." He admitted. "But I can't think of two better friends to be with, and I always learn so much when I'm around them."

Mina smiled. "Holmes is not the same man he once was."

Harry laughed. "Literally."

She smiled back at him. "I know it's silly to remark about that. But on some levels, I'm grateful for this..."

"New version?"

She didn't reply.

Harry sighed. "I will always miss the Holmes we all grew up with."

"As I, Harry. But he is no more." She hastily added. "At least in this particular universe. Who knows maybe when he..."

"Crossed over?" Harry asked.

"Yes. That sounds better. Crossed over. Maybe he did just like Conan has."

Harry looked sad for a moment. "Conan is special. He's always been special. I think more's at play with him being here than just...crossing over."

"Maybe so." Mina shot back. "But it gives us hope."

"Hope." Harry said, yet with another sigh.

Now that he wasn't all jubilant and bouncy as normal, his facial lines were becoming deeper and more obvious. "I think the weight of our war has finally reached my spirit."

She took his hands between hers. He resisted at first. But then relented. She clasped them tightly against her knees and leaned so close he felt as if her lips might touch him. "Harry, we must not. You must not...give up. It's a war we...this nation...our world...it cannot lose."

"Ghost Wars." He said, shaking his head.

"Occult Wars." She clarified.

He looked at her. "The demon was a ghost."

"Yes, but it would not have existed without someone using massive occult powers to stabilize its admission into our realm and projecting it."

"You know who is doing this?"

"I know what Ms. Hudson told me."

"That snitch." Harry said affectionately this time.

"Yes. But one we would all miss greatly if she were gone."

"Especially Watson."

"Speaking of whom." Watson interrupted, clearing his throat in embarrassment as he entered the sitting room, with Ms. Hudson at his heels.

They took seats near their friends.

"Ms. Hudson has appraised me of Mina's proposition, Harry, and I think you should take her up on it."

Harry gave Watson an angry look. "I don't like meddling in my affairs!"

Watson laughed. "Harry, since when? You've always meddled in ours...for better or worse as long as we've known each other."

Harry started to say something he would regret, then realized that Mina still had his hands. He gently pulled them away. He took a deep breath. "Does your father still have the remote underground chamber?"

"He does."

Harry thought about it a moment. "Very well. I will move into your house on one condition, Mina."

She gave him an angry look. "No. No conditions. We play honestly with each other; or we do not pay at all." She scalded him.

"Mina, I love you."

Mina all but melted at those words.

Watson and Ms. Hudson exchanged looks, slight smiles on their lips, but said nothing.

Harry rose and took Mina's hands in his. "I have been lying to myself for years now. Denying myself in the name of personal vanity and foolishness. Yes, I am the world's greatest magician..."

"Except for Merlin, of course." Mina reminded him with a slight smile.

"Yes, he. But...I need your support. I need..." He took another deep breath. His heart was racing like a fast Tesla car. "...You!"

"Well, now that's all settled." Holmes said as he entered the room, a slight smile on his lips and pipe in his right hand. "It's time we got down to business."

"Business?" Harry asked, his face filled with confusion.

Mina patted the chair next to her and he sat down, but he didn't let go of her hands. Never again!

Holmes took center stage in front of his friends, standing at the front of the fireplace, its warmth heating his backside. "I'm afraid this war has moved up another notch."

Harry hunched over. "That I will agree with."

"Not the demon, Harry. We can deal with demons."

"You mean I can."

"We...can." Holmes repeated, causing Harry to shut up, the scalding had done its work. Even though not overt.

Holmes waved his pipe like a University professor lecturing his students. "From now on we must assume that the enemy..."

"Enemy?" Harry asked.

"Yes." Holmes replied. "The true enemy."

"Harry, be quiet." Mina chided him.

"No, it's fine, Mina." Holmes spoke up. "We need his feedback, because he is going to be as heavily involved in what comes, even as all of us here."

Harry felt the weight that had been pulling him down suddenly left. "In what?"

"The Occult Wars."

Harry gave Holmes a blank look.

Holmes reached into his night robe and plucked out an envelope, sealed with the Royal seal. He handed it to Harry.

Harry looked up briefly at Holmes, who nodded. Harry broke the seal and read the message inside out loud.

"By order of Prince Churchill and his father, good King Andrew, the brotherhood of Baker Street shall be assisting our nation in combating this growing menace from the Germanies. The Verboten Party."

Harry looked up at Holmes. "Aren't they the ones connected to the Thames Shipyard murders?"

"Exactly."

Harry continued reading. "We, as a nation, can no longer tolerate just waiting for the next blow to fall. We must use every resource available to root out this subversive, and pervasive cult of terrorists. We shall not tolerate more deaths!"

Harry let out a low whistle. "This sounds very, very angry."

Watson laughed. "You should have seen Prince Churchill while he was writing it. Chomping on his cigar so hard, he bit it in half."

"Continuing to do so through an entire box, I might add." Holmes said.

"Amazing."

Harry continued reading the message again. "Therefore, as Prince and Commander of the Forces of our Britains, I do assign all merits, strengths, and powers to the Brotherhood of Baker Street to do so as they will to combat this new and growing force of terror and destruction."

Harry set the letter down in his lap. "This is a pretty tall order. How can a handful such as we are stop something as large as a continental war?"

Holmes eyes narrowed. "By rooting out the beast in the cellar."

Watson laughed. "Good one, Holmes."

Harry smiled. "I see. Take the war to them first."

Holmes said nothing.

Harry sighed, suddenly realizing the weight once more on his shoulders. "But without my magical equipment, I am virtually no better than anyone else here."

"I resent that, Harry." Watson snorted. "

"I mean, that my contribution is merely mortal then."

Mina spoke up. "Everyone here has such, Harry. Can't you see? We each must do what we can and what we can do best. And yes, I agree to your terms."

Harry stood up. "That won't be necessary. I will be staying here with my friends."

Watson and Ms. Hudson exchanged glances.

Holmes cleared his throat. "I, uh, made arrangements for your travel to the Count's home on the morrow."

Mina laughed. "Actually, you don't have to wait that long. I have a ride waiting outside. Since Harry has no valuables to bring, but himself, wonderful as it is, he can come at once."

Watson stood up and clapped his hands. "Splendid idea."

On Harry's look. "Uh, I mean, we shall miss you, Harry, of course, but you will be well taken care of. I've been assured of that."

Harry looked at everyone a long moment. "I never had a choice from the start, did I?"

Holmes said nothing. Everyone was silent.

Harry rolled his eyes. "Fine. I'll just go blow up the Count's dungeon instead."

Watson looked alarmed. "You were going to blow up things here?"

Harry turned to his friend. "Surely, you didn't think I could practice my magic, building up my arsenal again without some risk?"

Watson paled. He reached out a hand to Harry. "I wish you a speedy journey, Harry."

Everyone laughed.

Scotland Yard

Things have quieted down considerably since the demon flare up at Houdini's flat. Even the Inspector seems more relaxed than usual as he and his son, Constable Evans, a tall young man with reddish hair like his father's, but under better control, converse.

The front office is calm as well, with the Constables moving in and out of the building as they change shifts or come off them.

A prisoner, cuffed and waiting to be celled, sits patiently on a bench next to the Receiving Counter, where Sergeant O'Riley, a middle-aged man with a fine blonde handlebar mustache, calmly fills out the paperwork, while two bored Constables stand to the right and left of the prisoner, waiting to take him to his cell.

"Says here you were caught attempting to steal a map."

The prisoner looks up at the Sergeant. His eyes appear to be distant, almost blank. "Yes."

"Why?"

"Directions."

The Sergeant drilled his eyes into the man, searching to see if he could get more. "Just directions?"

"Directions."

"For what?"

The prisoner's eyes went all white and he began mumbling in a strange language.

"Hey Sarge!" The Constable hollered to the booking desk. "You recognize this guy's language?"

The Sarge came over and listened a moment. "Sounds like gibberish to me."

The prisoner suddenly smiled. "Tell the Inspector that I have a message for him."

The Constable and Sarge gave him a shocked look. He was looking at them, but his eyes were totally unfocused as if seeing another world.

"Why?" The Sarge demanded, his eyes narrowing suspiciously.

The prisoner just smiled.

"Why?" The Sarge insisted. "Tell me now or I'll have your sorry ass in jail for any number of charges!"

"What's wrong here, Sargeant?" The Inspector demanded as he passed by.

"This blaggart wants to speak with you but won't say why."

The prisoner looked at the Inspector. "I have a message for you."

"I'm listening." The Inspector said, humoring the man, because he looked a bit off. They ran into a lot of poor souls who just gave up and left reality to wherever it was they lived inside themselves.

The prisoner's voice changed, "You are to tell Mister Holmes that he's next."

Everyone fell back in surprise.

"What the...?" The Sergeant blasted out. "He sounds like one of those Germans."

The prisoner turned to look at the Sergeant. "That's because this miserable soul is not the real me. I would never make it that easy for you foolish, ignorant people!"

The Sergeant raised his voice. "Who you calling...?"

The Inspector touched the Sergeant on his shoulder and put him behind him. "Why should I tell him anything at all?"

The prisoner looked up at the Inspector. "Because death calls from the skies!"

Then the prisoner made choking sounds.

"Get us a medic!" Hollered the Inspector as the prisoner began shaking violently, froth coming from his mouth.

A medic rushed from the back area for the prisoner, but by that time his head had fallen onto his chest, and a gush of blood had poured out.

The medic took the man's head and lifted it. He opened the bloody mouth. "He's bitten off his own tongue and swallowed it!"

221B

Holmes was the first out of his room at the sound of a siren from outside. He went to the window in time to spot the Inspector climbing from his wagon, followed by Constable Evans. Both men looked dragged out.

Watson came out, rubbing his eyes. "My God! Don't we ever get a chance to rest around here?"

A pounding came on the front door.

Ms. Hudson was heard several moments later opening the door.

Inspector Bloodstone and his son, Constable Evans, came into the sitting room.

"Holmes, we need you!" The Inspector said before anyone could greet him or ask any questions.

Holmes, who was already dressed, slipped on his overcoat and deerstalker cap, then headed for the stairs.

"Coming Watson?"

Scotland Yard Morgue

"And you say the man was arrested for trying to steal a map?" Holmes inquired of the Constable who had brought him in.

The man looked uncomfortable standing next to the dead prisoner, who was laid out on a steel gurney, his chest cut open, and body parts deposited in a steel container next to the gurney.

"Aye, Sir. And strange it was too. He kept trying to get past me, to break free and go back and take it again, even though I was willing to just let him go. He wouldn't take no for an answer. The shop keeper didn't want to charge him; just wanted him gone. He was scaring the both of us, he was."

"I see."

Holmes turned to look as Watson began sawing open the bone of the man's brainpan. The grinding sound was loud.

The Constable paled and looked ready to throw up.

"One last question, Constable."

"Yes, Mister Holmes."

"Which map?"

The Constable couldn't wait any longer; he clasped a hand over his mouth, made loud gagging sounds as Watson pulled the prisoner's brain out and laid it in an open pain, where it made a huge sticky sound, like fresh meat on a skillet.

Constable Evans entered as the man was fleeing. He spotted Holmes and angled to him, avoiding several other bodies on gurneys, with sheets on t hem.

"Holmes, the Inspector said you might want this." He held out a map.

Holmes took the map and perused its contents. "Interesting."

"Tell the Inspector that Watson and I are almost done. I'm afraid we'll have to discuss this at some length, but I shall make sure we return in the morning to complete our report."

Watson grunted. "Sure, and that's not going to happen. It's only an hour to dawn."

He wiped at his face, smearing it with blood and grinned. "Bloody business this."

Holmes smiled.

The Map Shop

Captain Byrnes entered the Map Shop cautiously, not knowing what to expect. The place was quite dark for a store that sold reading documents. He searched the aisles, where numerous maps were on display, including atlases, then spotted Holmes and Watson at the sales counter speaking to someone.

Holmes turned around and spotted him. "This way, Captain, if you please."

The Captain wove through the tangled aisles of maps and books and joined the detective and his partner. "Sorry, I'm late. Prince Charles called me to a meeting this morning with the Cabinet."

"How is his father doing?"

"The old buzzard's tough as a bull. He'll be fine." Captain Byrnes replied, with the hint of a smile. "Like son, like father, you know."

Holmes humored his quaint joke with a faint smile, then turned to the Shop Manager. "This is Mister Giles. Mister Giles, Captain Byrnes of the M.I.12."

Mister Giles gave Holmes a blank look.

The Captain smiled and offered his hand. Mister Giles took it. "It stands for Military Intelligence 12th Unit."

"Oh." Mister Giles said.

"So, what is so important that you interrupt a top cabinet meeting with the Prince?"

Watson walked away and began looking at other maps while his friend spoke to the Captain.

"It seems that the prisoner we spoke about is connected to the assassination attempt."

"But how? A map?"

Holmes spread the map out. It was of Buckingham Palace.

28

"Everyone buys them things." Mister Giles noted.

"Yes, but how many copies in a store have this marked?" Holmes pointed out, stabbing a finger in the exact spot that the gardener's hut was located, circled in a rough pencil mark.

"Mister Giles, if you would please."

Mister Giles poured a box of similar maps on the counter.

Holmes opened a second map to the same place. Again, the mark around the gardener's hut. He repeated this about three more times, when the Captain stopped him by putting his hand over the next one.

The Captain eyed Holmes thoughtfully. "You're telling me that that man, the one who choked to death on his own tongue. He did all this?"

"Yes, Captain." Holmes replied.

Mister Giles nodded. "That's why I called for help. I was afraid he wouldn't stop at making circles on maps but might decide to start marking them around me!"

The Captain sighed. "This case just keeps getting more and more stranger."

"Indeed, it does." Homes agreed.

Watson made a startled sound.

Holmes and the Captain rushed over.

Watson was pointing to a mark on one of the racks. "Wasn't this where all those maps came from?"

Mister Giles peered over their shoulders. "Exactly! I say, what's that mark doing there?"

He gave Holmes a frightened look. "It wasn't there earlier."

"Has anyone come in since the incident. Stood in that spot?" Holmes inquired, his eyes burning feverishly with energy.

Mister Giles shook his head. "The Inspector insisted that no one come into the shop until all the evidence was gathered; and then when I was about to open again; news came of the poor sod's death, and I was told to hold it closed yet longer."

He turned to the Captain. 'You can tell His Majesty, that I'm co-operating as best I can, but this is costing me a lot of business."

The Captain smiled. "Don't worry, I'm sure the Prince will make it up to you. He's the good sort."

Mister Giles breathed a sigh of relief. "Very well then. Anything else I can help you gentlemen with?"

"Yes." Holmes said.

Mister Giles looked at Holmes.

Death From the Skies

Holmes, the Inspector, Constable Evans, Watson, and Captain Byrnes sat about the fireplace, sipping at tea, quietly ruminating over the facts they had just finished discussing.

"And you say the prisoner said..." Holmes cued Constable Evans.

"I wasn't there, but father said something like, ' death calls from the skies.'"

Holmes sat back in his chair and put his chin on his right fist, considering what he had been told.

Watson looked worried. "You don't think they're going to try that demon thing again, do you, Holmes?"

"No. And that's what worries me. If not that, then what?" Holmes replied, his eyes distant.

Captain Byrnes seemed relaxed, though a bit tense in the shoulders, as if he were holding something back.

Holmes looked over at him. "You've been quiet, Captain. What's on your mind?"

"When you said death from the skies, it brought to mind several things."

"Such as?"

The Captain leaned closer. "We have it on the highest authority..."

"Spies." The Inspector said.

Captain Byrnes glanced at him. "Yes. But they would know."

"Know what, Captain. And I would thank you, Inspector, to please refrain from remarks until I'm ready to hear them."

The Inspector's face turned red. He was about to blast Holmes, when Constable put a hand on his father's arm and shook his head. The Inspector instead got up and went to the window to look out over Baker Street. He looked up and watched the skies.

"Know what, Captain?" Holmes encouraged the Captain.

"There's some sort of super weapon that the Verboten Party has launched."

"Super weapon?" Watson blurted out. "Besides demons, we now have to worry about flying bombs and all that nonsense?"

The Captain gave Watson a surprised look. "Even you and Holmes don't have that high of a security clearance to know about them!"

Holmes leaned forward. "Captain, lives are at stake."

The Captain sighed, closed his eyes, and nodded. "Our top man lost his life getting this information to us." He looked up and gave everyone a warning look. "This must not leave this building!"

When he saw that everyone had agreed with a nod of the ear, a blink of the eye, or a gesture, he went on. "As you probably already know from good King Andrew; the Verboten Party has been arming itself. In advance of that arming they have begun a lengthy and well-planned series of sabotage."

"The Thames Construction site being one of them." Holmes noted.

"Yes. And Harry's flat."

"But why Harry?" Holmes asked, a bit perplexed at first.

"Isn't it obvious?"

Watson blurted out what Holmes had already deduced. "Harry's our secret weapon to defeat their occult powers."

"Exactly." Captain Byrnes replied.

Holmes smiled at Watson. "Very good, Watson. My exact thoughts. So, if they could kill both Harry and the Prince...."

"And now you!" The Captain added.

Watson paled. "That's ghastly."

"No, Watson. It's war." Holmes commented.

"I hear something." The Inspector called to them.

Captain Byrnes smiled. "We have dirigibles flying overhead to block any kind of aerial attack on this place."

"No, it's not the sound of a dirigible. I'd recognize that sound."

Watson hurried to the window and flung it full open.

Everyone went totally silent.

Captain Byrnes stuck his head out the window. He listened a moment, then looked back inside. "Everyone out of here! Now!"

Watson was first one down the stairs. He pounded on Ms. Hudson's door as the others flew past him to the street. Holmes waited for his friend.

"Go on! She just must slip something on!"

Holmes refused to move.

Watson turned on him. "For God's sake man, are you deaf?"

Holmes rushed outside.

Suddenly, the front door slammed shut on its own.

Watson gave it a surprised look. He went to it, tried to open it. It wouldn't budge.

Ms. Hudson came out wearing an overcoat and scarf. "What's wrong, John?'

"Air raid! Blast it the door won't open!"

Dragons of Death

Holmes snapped around when the front door slammed shut. He immediately went to it to reopen it. It wouldn't budge.

"Watson, open up!"

"I can't!" Watson cried through the door. "It won't budge!"

The sound from the skies became louder and louder.

"Holmes get away from there. Now!" Captain Byrnes ordered.

Holmes looked on helplessly at the door and then noticed something on its lower right front.

"Now!"

Constable Evans and Captain Byrnes both ran up, bodily grabbed Holmes, who struggled to break free, and dragged him towards the nearest alley, where Captain Byrnes and the Inspector dashed.

They were just about into the alley when all hell broke loose and a pair of buzz bombs, shaped like ancient Chinese dragons descended on trails of fire straight towards 221 Baker Street.

Holmes finally broke free. He spun about just as the two flying bombs dropped past the rooftops into view.

221B Baker Street

Holmes snapped around when the Baker Street front door slammed shut. He immediately went to it to reopen it. It wouldn't.

"Watson, open up!"

"I can't!" Watson cried through the door. "It won't budge!"

The sound from the skies became louder and louder.

"Holmes get away from there. Now!" Captain Byrnes ordered.

Holmes looked on helplessly at the door and then noticed something on its lower right front.

"Wait, I've found something." Holmes hollered.

Constable Evans and Captain Byrnes both ran up, bodily grabbed Holmes, who struggled to break free, and dragged him towards the nearest alley, where Captain Byrnes and the Inspector dashed. "You must let me go!" Holmes shouted.

They ignored him.

Holmes stomped on Captain Byrnes's right foot. The man howled in pain. Holmes elbowed the constable at the same time, who then doubled over in pain.

Holmes dashed for the front porch of 221B as fast as he could. He dropped to a knee, pulled out a key and began frantically scratching at the marking he had discovered on the lower right of the front door.

"Holmes!"

"Shut up, Watson, I'm saving you!" He hollered at the door.

The sound in the sky grew ear shattering.

Holmes pressed too hard on the key, and it spun from his hand into the air and out of reach. He did the only thing he could; he began scratching at the mark, breaking his fingernails, and causing his fingertips to bleed profusely from the splinters he gouged away from the wood.

Holmes suddenly realized the buzzing sound had ceased. He looked away from the door.

Constable Evans and the Captain looked on from the alleyway in horror as two buzz bombs, shaped like ancient Chinese dragons blasted into view on Baker Street.

Dragons in the Sky

Sherlock Holmes shut his eyes.

"I'm sorry, Watson." He uttered, knowing he would not be heard.

What must be he would accept. Then he heard a familiar sound. He opened his eyes to look at the street as a Tesla slammed on its brakes and Harry Houdini leaped from behind the wheel and held a hand up towards the buzz bombers. "NO!"

A powerful field of magic gathered around his fist and his body and began expanding.

Holmes saw the magic leaping towards him; enfold him and the buildings nearest to him.

Suddenly, the buzz bombers veered off and shot straight into the heavens.

An explosion shattered the night. So large and bright, the entire city block was lit up as brightly as if the sun had freshly risen above the rooftops.

Not even Harry's magic could stop the impact of the shrapnel from striking his car, him, and the buildings about him.

Holmes was struck on his right shoulder and slammed against the door, the same time as it opened.

"Holmes!" Watson cried out, not realizing his friend was laying on the porch at first. "The door suddenly opened of its own free will."

"Sherlock!" Watson uttered as he saw his friend lying before him unconscious.

Ms. Hudson came out behind him and then rushed around him and to the side of Holmes. She hollered at Captain Byrnes and the Inspector

Captain Byrnes rushed to the porch, alongside Constable Evans, who helped him and Watson lift Holmes in their arms, as gently as if carrying a baby.

Watson felt his friend's neck. "He's alive! Hurry! Take him upstairs."

"They might try again." Captain Byrnes warned.

Harry, who had rushed to the steps, shook his head. He was looking at the mark on the door. "They won't find it so easily this time. Holmes destroyed their spell."

Watson noticed the bleeding fingertips on both of Holmes' hands. "Dear God! His fingers!"

Harry looked at the door, then Holmes. He looked at Watson. "I wondered why they were so easily deflected."

Constable Evans gave him a confused look. "But you blew them up!"

"No. I only told them to stop." He looked at Holmes and smiled gently. "This man confused them. They blew finally because they were on a timer."

"And time ran out." Constable Evans remarked.

"Yes. And fortunately for you three." He looked at Watson, Ms. Hudson, and Holmes. "He broke the master spell on the door."

Constable Evans looked at the scratch marks on the door, then at Holmes' bleeding fingers. "They can do that? They can curse a door to bring bombs to it?"

"Guys!" Ms. Hudson complained.

"Oh my God!" Watson declared. "Come, Constable, we must hurry Holmes to the hospital at once!"

THEY HURRIED TO THE Constable's wagon, which still had still debris burning on its rooftop.

Constable Evans slid Holmes all the way into Watson's arms, then hurriedly cleaned the roof, which still smoked from the heart of the objects, then opened the back for Watson to slide Holmes inside.

But Watson didn't do that, instead he carefully climbed inside, keeping Holmes cradled in his arms.

Watson looked at Holmes with sad eyes. "Somehow our lives are never simple, are they, Holmes?"

Ms. Hudson climbed in the other side and cradled Holmes' head in her lap. She looked over at Watson and touched his arm. "He's going to be fine, John."

Constable Evans put the car into gear, and they took off, the siren wailing as they drove.

"This time." Watson uttered, almost choking. "What about the next, or the next, or the...?"

Ms. Hudson put a finger to his mouth. "Let the next time take care of itself. He's alive and he's going to survive. We're going to survive." She told him, putting a lot of emotional energy into the word "we."

HARRY, FEELING AS RAGGED as he looked turned to Captain Byrnes. "It would seem the Occult Wars have fully begun."

Captain Byrnes frowned. "And we are yet again on the receiving end of it, with no target in sight to retaliate against."

Harry shook his head, eyeing the destruction about them as fire engines, sirens wailing, began slamming into view.

"I suspect you're going to get your chance sooner than you think."

The Captain gave Harry an appraising look.

"Captain, I need to finish what Holmes started. Please excuse me."

Harry kneeled before the door and held his hand over the bloodied mark on it.

He shut his eyes.

The Captain didn't see what happened next, he was too busy running into the street to guide the firemen who were leaping from braking fire trucks.

221B Baker Street

Holmes laid on his bed, covered by a warmer, a cool cloth on his forehead, a compress on his right shoulder. He looked weary. More so than he felt, however.

For a few brief moments he saw a vision of the woman he had lost. Not the one who died in his arms, but the one who got away. Moriarty's daughter. Destiny.

"Who's Destiny?" Captain Byrnes asked in the void where Holmes stood within his mind.

Holmes turned towards the disembodied voice. "Someone dear to me."

"She's Professor Moriarty's daughter." Watson replied for Holmes.

Holmes squinted into the darkness around him. As he did, he saw a vague shape move from the deeper shadows towards him. As the form neared, he could tell it was female and a tall one. Almost as tall as he.

Her face was veiled so he could only see her eyes. But they were eyes he would never forget as long as he lived. That is, if he were still alive.

"I've missed you." He told her.

She laughed. "I told you I was your Destiny."

He smiled. "Everyone's my destiny these days."

She came closer and looked into his eyes. "I'm sorry for any pain I've brought to you."

"I never believed for one moment that you truly meant to." He told her.

She came closer still until he could smell the scent of Sandalwood on her. "We will meet again soon. You will need me. And when you do. I will be there for you."

Holmes smiled gently at her. "If only this weren't a dream, I might even believe that lie."

She looked hurt for a moment, and then laughed. "Believe it or not. Your choice, Holmes!"

Then she vanished and Holmes eyes opened to stare at Watson, who was giving him a worried look.

"You're back."

"Who's Destiny?" Captain Byrnes asked yet again.

Holmes didn't reply. Watson didn't either. He knew full well who Destiny was. A very strong willed, powerful, and intelligent woman, whose beauty encompassed Holmes' in ways Watson hadn't seen in a long time, if ever. Professor Moriarty's daughter. She had once sought revenge against Holmes; but instead had fallen madly in love with him.

Watson mused how strange the path of destiny had taken the very real Destiny and he suspected she felt no less, were she still alive somewhere.

"We thought we lost you for a time, Holmes." Watson worriedly told Holmes.

Holmes looked into his eyes and smiled gently. He struggled to sit up. He felt lancing pains shooting down into his feet. "I thought I had lost me as well."

Watson was shoved aside, and Captain Byrnes looked at Holmes. "How did you know what that mark was?"

"Captain, let him rest!" Watson warned.

"This is war. We need all the information we can get." Captain Byrnes almost shouted into Watson's face.

Watson stepped into Captain Byrnes face and glared at him. "You ever try anything like that again with me, Captain, and you shall have your war...immediately!"

"Boys!" Ms. Hudson cried out. She stepped between them, causing Captain Byrnes to back off, embarrassed at her closeness.

Watson didn't budge though. He remained rooted at the side of Holmes; his hands balled into fists, his eyes angry lumps of coal in his face.

Captain Byrnes looked ready to fight as well.

"If you two boys don't stop that right now, I'm going to return with a broom and turn you over my knees!"

Captain Byrnes and Watson both gave her surprised looks.

She put her hands on her hips to emphasize she meant it.

Captain Byrnes nodded to her, gave Watson one last scowl, then hurried from the room.

Watson gave Ms. Hudson a little hurt boy look and exited.

Ms. Hudson sat down beside Holmes and changed the damp cloth she had placed over his forehead to help reduce his fever. She replaced it with the warm one she had brought in from the kitchen. "Better now?"

"You're a good soul, Ms. Hudson."

"I know." She giggled.

She got up.

"Captain Byrnes is going to walk like a mouse around you from now on." Holmes said, his voice weak and fading away.

Went to the Tesla lamp by the door and switched it off. "There will be plenty of time in the morning to talk about everything."

"But I feel fine." Holmes responded, struggling to sit up again. He didn't make it. He slid back down under his covers and his head tilted to the side.

Ms. Hudson didn't hear Watson return into the room, but she felt his warm hands as they came to rest on her shoulders. She nuzzled back against him, absorbing his reassuring presence.

"I worry about you all so much."

"I know you do."

"He needs his rest now."

"Yes. And that's why I slipped him a sedative when he wasn't paying attention. He's so stubborn at times."

Ms. Hudson turned into Watson's embrace and smiled. She touched his nose gently with a forefinger. "And who else do we know like that."

Watson gave her a kiss on her forehead.

"I suppose that would be me."

"That's what makes the two of you such a fine fit." She teased. "You're both stubborn as oxen."

He smiled. "In that case. Guilty as charged, my dear."

She smiled warmly. "I know. Now shoo! Let him rest!"

She gently pushed Watson from the room, even as he strove to get just one more look at his hurt friend, and then she left also, shutting the door behind her.

Holmes slid into a troubled sleep, with nightmarish images of dead people, ghost-like figures, and long-lost friends and companions. His face looked more and more troubled as he did so. He began sweating profusely, his face flushing. Tiny moans escaped his lips.

A trembling of the air and a brightening near his bed started and for a brief time a feminine figure stood beside him, silent and watching. She leaned over, gently kissed his forehead and then his lips.

Holmes' mutterings stopped. His face relaxed. He became peaceful.

She smiled, and then gradually faded away until only the darkness remained once more.

Council of War

Watson, Captain Byrnes, the Inspector and Constable Evans sat near the fireplace, bathing in its war glow, palms holding cups of tea.

Their thoughts were wandering through the events that had led to this moment when the front door had a loud knocking on it.

"Come in!" They heard Ms. Hudson.

Several moments later, Harry, Conan and Professor Challenger entered the room.

Challenger looked at the dining table and grinned. It was heaped with fresh scones, alongside a steaming tea pot.

"Don't mind if I do." He invited himself and quickly poured a cup of tea and took six of the scones onto a napkin as Watson watched him with a scowl.

"Good morning, Watson. Great day, isn't it?"

Watson grunted and looked away.

Conan smiled. Those two were always at each other's throats. And not just over the scones, though that was a major source of aggravation for Watson, who was a bit proprietary about them and who ate them and how many.

He poured tea for himself and sat next to Watson. "How is he doing? We came as fast as we could once Harry notified us."

"A minor fracture and blood loss. A few days rest will heal most of it, but I'm afraid his shoulder is going to bother him for a while." Watson replied.

"Perhaps. But knowing Holmes as I do." He paused for Watson to nod. "And you do." Watson nodded once more. "I find it highly unlikely he will stay in bed more than this night, if even that."

Watson laughed. "You know my friend like an open book."

Conan just smiled at the reference to having been the original creator of Holmes in his own world.

Harry sat down next to them, cradling a cup of tea in his hands. "It was a close call. If Holmes hadn't altered that ward...it was the symbol, he had been scratching away at...placed there to attract the buzz bombers they would have struck sooner, and I would have been too late to stop them."

"So, the slight alteration, confused them, but didn't stop them. Why?" Challenger asked.

Harry shrugged. "Magic is unique. Occult magic is layered in more complicated ways than just plain potion magic, which I and Merlin excel at."

"I see." Challenger noted. "Then this magic is more thought orientated?"

Harry gave Challenger a look of appreciation. "Very good, Challenger. Yes. It uses a physical base like mine but goes a step further with mental direction. Hence occult, rather than just simple magic."

Captain Byrnes looked over. "Yet you were able to deflect those bombs with a gesture from your hand. I thought your magic was limited now."

"It is."

Captain Byrnes whistled. "If that's what it's like when it's limited, I'd hate to be on the receiving end of it when it wasn't."

Harry smiled and looked at Watson again.

"You know they'll try again, don't you?"

The Inspector spoke up. "Not on my watch!"

Constable Evans smiled. "Father they can control minds. Who's to say one of our own men won't do something they would regret?" Constable Evans looked miserable when he said the rest of his words. "Maybe even one of us."

The Inspector started to say something, then shut up. "Blasted occult stuff is going to drive me out of business or my mind." Then he realized what he was saying and gave Constable Evans, his son, a horrified look. "Dear God in heaven!"

"You see what I mean," Constable Evans said.

"Unfortunately. All too clearly," The Inspector replied, now growing pensive as he considered the ramifications of what they were discussing.

Harry smiled at him. "Don't worry, Inspector. We're going to solve this just fine."

Watson perked up, "You have an idea?"

"Does he ever not?" Challenger blasted from his side of the fireplace. "Harrys like a ball of snow that rolls down a hill and just keeps getting bigger and bigger."

Captain Byrnes gave Harry a thoughtful look. "You'd better be, because from what Winston told me..."

"Winston?" Harry asked. "Who's Winston?"

"The Prince, Harry." Challenger informed him.

"Oh!" Harry uttered. "That Winston."

He looked back at the Captain, who went on. "What is coming is going to get worse than anything we can possibly ever imagine."

"Oh, I don't know, Captain, I can imagine a whole lot of things."

The Captain's look shut him up.

And that's not an easy thing to do with Harry.

The Underground Fortress

Commander Kepfler smashed his metallic fist onto his desk, shattering it in two.

People scattered away from the sudden outburst, alarm on their faces.

He turned towards Scar, his face ugly like a feral beast. "You told me you placed the mark securely!"

"I did," Scar retorted, anger at the accusations barely held back.

Commandant Kepfler stormed towards him, until he was looking down into Scar's face. "I suppose you will blame this on one of my men again?"

"No." Scar replied.

That took the steam out of the Commandant's anger. "What?"

"We are just underestimating our opponents."

Commandant Kepfler stepped away from Scar.

"Explain?"

Scar gave the Commandant a scornful look. "I thought you center-worlders knew more than that? All your psychic powers, your extraordinary machinery, and you still don't know how to understand the drive of a single man."

"We have pushed Herr Himmler into power."

"With his consent."

"Perhaps."

Scar filed that information in the back of his mind and went on. "221B, Commandant. That is the center of your problem. The men who live there are the driving force of the resistance to our efforts. Everyone else is just incompetent fools compared to that lot."

He smirked. "Perhaps, even...ourselves."

Commandant Kepfler scowled at Scar, who hurriedly backed out of the Commandant's reach. He waved a hand. "To defeat fire, you must also use fire. You are using too much force!"

"There can never be too much force!"

Scar smiled, knowing what he would say next would either kill him or win his argument.

"Then why is it that your people live hidden inside our planet for safety, and we rule the earth's surface with impunity?"

Scar waited to see if he would live through the next five seconds or make the point he was striving for. It was going to be a long wait.

Everyone tensed, expecting the worst.

The Commandant raised his metal fist to strike.

Scar sighed. Death it was then.

Recovery

Watson fretted in the sitting room, as Ms. Hudson began setting the table for six. She laid out a beautiful set of napkins she had embroidered with silver leaves, a set of silverware with tiny red roses on their handles and plates of China with silver leaves and red roses on their edges.

"You're quiet, John." She said, as she laid out napkins with silver leaves on their edges next to the plates. She had sewn those as well. Quite a creative woman.

He sighed, then came over and helped her set up the rest of the table. "I don't like it is all."

"And you think anyone else does?"

He shrugged. "You know me too well, Martha."

"Yes. And I love you all the more because of it."

He stopped setting cups next to plates when her hand found his. He looked into her eyes. Those wonderful eyes that went deep into her soul, the warmth and depth of her character smiling out at him with the sincerity of a small child and the innocence of an angel. He always melted inside when she did that. He felt his fears and doubts melting in a swirl of warmth she always gave him without restraint.

"I love you."

"And I love you more." She teased.

He grinned and gave her a quick peck on the cheek.

"Oh, that will never do." She told him in a teasing voice.

He grinned wider and took her face in his hands and gave her a long kiss.

"Ah-hem!" Challenger said, clearing his throat rather loudly as he entered.

Watson and Ms. Hudson hurriedly pulled apart.

"Too late I'm afraid." Conan told them as he leaned against the entrance next to Challenger, arms crossed and grinning widely.

Watson scowled at them. "Who let you in?"

"I." Holmes replied as he ascended into view and stepped into the room.

He was dressed lightly, just a shirt, slacks, and a light cap. Not his usual deerstalker one. He smiled.

"Feeling better then?"

"By halves."

"I didn't hear you get up this morning."

Ms. Hudson pinched Watson's right cheek. "That's because you snore so loudly you can't even hear yourself thinking, dear."

He glared at her. "How would you know that?"

Everyone turned to look at Ms. Hudson, who just smiled, her face lit with an obvious answer all the men in the room could read quite clearly. She brushed past Holmes, giving him a light smile as she passed.

Challenger turned to watch her descend to her apartment. "Remarkable woman, Watson. If she were available..."

"But she is not." Watson cut him off decisively.

Holmes laughed.

Conan grinned. "I'm glad at least one of us sees the humor in that." He teased.

They all sat down at the table, except for Holmes, who went to the window to look out.

"I had the strangest dream last night." He told his friends.

"Which was?" Challenger asked first.

"That someone from my past was in my room."

Watson looked alarmed. "Not Moriarty again?"

Holmes looked to his friend, an amused look on his face. "Close."

Watson faltered for a moment. "Her!"

"Indeed." Holmes decreed.

He clasped his hands behind his back and walked back and forth across the room, gathering his thoughts.

"I think this war has increased more than just a little, my friends."

The front door below was banged upon. Ms. Hudson greeted someone, and they hurried up the stairs.

"I hope I'm not too late." Harry uttered as he entered. It's a bit far from the Count's place."

"You must have flown to get here so fast, Harry." Challenger noted.

Harry said nothing. He didn't want to speak of the horrid flight through the air that the Count Dracula had given him. He had never felt so embarrassed or humiliated in his life to be carried like a small child in that powerful man's arms.

He took a seat at the table.

There were now five men in the room. One seat remained.

Holmes glanced at Harry and nodded. "It's good of you to come, Harry. I was counting on it."

"Feeling any better, Holmes?"

"Yes. Much. Thank you," Holmes replied, though it was obvious his shoulder still hurt by the way he would wince every so often when he moved it.

Harry nodded. Holmes would never complain. It wasn't his nature.

Holmes grimaced as he touched his right shoulder. "Least it works, if a bit damnably." He noted with the hint of a smile.

"If not for your quick thinking, Holmes, Ms. Hudson and I would have died." Watson pointed out.

"This reminds me." Conan interrupted. "How did you know what to do?"

Holmes smiled. "Harry is a good teacher."

Harry grinned and raised a hand in acknowledgement.

"When I first noted the mark on the door, I thought it nothing more than a scuffle, but as the good Captain dragged me away to safety I remembered where I had seen that mark before."

"My house." Harry announced proudly.

"Indeed." Holmes replied. "Even though the one on your house was seriously marred. It was clear enough that it had been placed there for a reason.

"And?" Harry added.

Holmes smiled at him. "You told me what it meant."

"Indeed." Harry teased.

Holmes barked with laughter.

The tension in the room lightened. Everyone was worried that Holmes was in worse shape than he commented, but now they knew he was better. He seldom laughed.

Ms. Hudson came up the stairs, a huge silver tray in her arms. "Glad to see you young men enjoying yourselves."

Watson and Challenger both rushed over to help her. She let go and they carried the tray to the table and set it down.

Watson gave Challenger a scowl but said nothing as Challenger assisted in distributing bowls of food for their consumption.

Ms. Hudson hurried back downstairs and came back up quickly with two steaming pots. One of coffee and one of tea. She set them on the table and then took the sixth chair at the table and beamed proudly at Watson, who was managing his temper quite well, despite Challenger doing the best he could to stir it up.

Finally, all food on the table, Challenger and Watson sat down. Challenger next to Conan. Watson between Ms. Hudson and Holmes. Harry to the other side of Challenger and Holmes.

"Harry, would you like to do the honors?" Ms. Hudson asked.

Harry bowed his head and put hands on the table. Everyone took a hand and bowed their heads.

"Dear God, who art in Heaven, please take pity on we poor hungry souls and forgive us for wanting to eat right away. Amen!"

Everyone broke into laughter and began adding food to their plates.

The Dead

"Why are we here?" Scar demanded as six of his fellow Verbotens dug at old graves in the cemetery. "We've driven for miles and miles. At least give us a clue as to what is going on, Commandant."

Commandant Kepfler eyed the open graves. "We are recruiting."

"Dead people? Nothing more than husks. How can they be of any use?"

Commandant Kepfler gave Scar a condescending smile. "God is not the only one who can give life."

Scar shook his head at the mysterious and obviously blasphemous statement and went to help one of his fellows as he slipped a harness about a newly revealed coffin. He dropped in beside him and angled the harness so that it snagged onto the old box.

He wrinkled his nose. "Must be a leak. Stinks to hell and back."

Reinhardt, his companion in the grave, nodded his head. "Like schiess it smells."

"Very, very old one!" Scar agreed.

"Okay!" He hollered from the hole.

He and Reinhardt crawled from the hole and stood up to watch as two others began tugging on the small lift they had rigged over the grave site.

Commandant Kepfler watched silently from the rear.

They grunted at the effort of moving the heavy box, especially when they had to swing it over to land evenly on the nearby ground.

But they managed it.

They then went to the next gravesite and repeated the same thing as two men in that hole harnessed the grave box and then helped them to shift it from the grave.

It took them the better part of the day and into the night to complete their work. They all collapsed against an old mausoleum, striving to catch their breaths and their strengths once they were done.

Scar broke out a bag and pulled bottled beers from it. He passed them around. Even one to the Commandant, who nodded in thanks.

"Now what, Commandant?"

The Commandant finished his beer in one swig, belched very loudly, and then tossed his bottle into the nearest gravesite.

He eyed the dozen coffins lying on the ground.

"We wait."

Watching and Waiting

She watched from behind a small grove of trees as the Germans finished their beers, her eyes especially focused on the Commandant.

Once he peered back in her direction, as if feeling her presence, but then he looked away again and continued chatting with his people.

She smiled and then began withdrawing from the graveyard.

She reached the nearby park and made her way swiftly through it, as curls of mist began to gather in the night on the sidewalk that was swiftly beginning to become wet from the moisture. She paused once to listen, her eyes alert. She shook her head, as if trying to clear it, pulled the veil she wore across her face higher and her scarf tighter about her throat. No time to get distracted she thought to herself and completed her short hike through the park, where a vehicle sat at the curb.

She climbed into the back and knocked on the driver compartment. The vehicle swung out into the lane and began moving faster and faster.

"Much to be done." She commented.

"Agreed." A male voice replied from opposite her. He leaned into the weak light of the cabin, revealing James Moriarty, the duplicate Moriarty who had escaped Victorian London of his world, accidentally killing the Moriarty of this world. Her father.

"What next?" He asked gently.

She looked at him a long time. "You are so much different from my father."

"And so much younger as well, I might add." He responded with a warm grin.

She stared at his face a long time in thought, and then nodded. "And younger. This would explain how you are so much different. Father was not always a twisted man."

"None are born that way, Destiny." James replied gently. "But we choose our paths, rightly or wrongly, and then must live or die by those choices."

"And what of what I just saw?" She asked.

"For now. Nothing."

"But Holmes..."

He cut her off. "Will be safe."

"But..."

"I swear to you I will make sure of that." He told her.

She searched his eyes. "I don't believe in fairy tales."

He smiled. "And that's why we are working together now."

"For now." She agreed.

"For now." He nodded. "For now."

"But what if one day I mean harm to your friend?" She asked him.

James laughed.

"What if?" She demanded, growing more and more furious with his laughter.

James laughed even harder.

Finally, she could stand it no longer and turned away from him, shutting him out with her own thoughts, which drifted away immediately to the man she lived without, but longed to be with again. The one and only man she had ever truly given her heart to. Sherlock Holmes!

The Dungeon

Harry paced the dungeon chamber he had set up for his magic experiments. It was not a horrible place, but it was further away from Baker Street than he liked. Had these been ordinary times, he might have relented on some of his worries, but after the recent occult attacks, he could no longer just say it wasn't going to happen.

It was happening. And sooner than he had hoped and worse than he had thought it would be. And with dire consequences. He hadn't told anyone, but he still barely had use of his hand after the conjuring he had done. The negative energies of the buzz bombers had been so powerful that his hand had been burnt severely by the battle between his powers and that of the dark force.

Not something visible to the eyes of others, but to himself, as he stood there with his hand raised to resist that terrible force unleashed on Baker Street, he had seen the malevolent energies, not as bombs about to ignite, but rather as fierce demons whose sole intent was to maim and destroy.

It had been close.

Too close.

He rubbed some more healing balm on his burnt hand when a voice caught his attention from behind.

"Harry."

A tender voice he recognized immediately.

He turned away from the magic potion he had been mixing carefully in a silver pewter and rushed over to take Mina's hands as she descended the last steps into his "man cave" beneath the ground as she nicknamed it.

He kissed both her hands and she gave him a smile, raised her lips for him to kiss as well. He didn't need to be encouraged any further. He immediately took the plunge, allowing her warmth to seep into him, soothing his growing sense of discomfort he had been feeling these last twenty-four hours.

Finally, he tilted back again, and she withdrew from his arms. He smiled into her lovely face. "I don't know which I've missed more. My magic or you," He teased.

She laughed. Ignored his taunt and went to his table where the potion was boiling away.

"You've been making progress, I see."

"I have."

She turned slowly about, taking in the changed look of the old dungeon room. "It looks almost cheerful."

He had placed vases of flowers every few feet to offset the odor of decay that had seeped into the walls and floor of the chamber.

He had also liberally sprinkled wax of cinnamon and honeysuckle leaves across the floor to absorb the ranker odors.

So, it was beginning to smell...almost livable.

She turned back to him. Smiling. "I could almost think that you weren't just teasing me after seeing all this."

He laughed and took her into his arms again, nuzzling her neck with his lips.

She sighed languorously, clutching at him with her hands on his face. She looked up into his eyes. He smiled.

He looked her over slowly.

"Harry. Father would kill you if he caught you doing that."

"And will you...kill me?" He asked her, gently leading her towards a room that opened off the chamber, where a very lovely down bed awaited.

"Maybe." She teased, eyeing the bed he was leading her towards. She threw him down on the bed and jumped on him. "Afterwards."

THEY LAY THERE A LONG time afterwards, both still sweaty from their love making. He gently draped an arm about her waist and drew her close to him, loving the feel of her silky flesh against his own.

He began nibbling on the pink rosettes of her nipples and she let out a small cry and grabbed him hard.

"I hope I'm not interrupting anything?" Count Dracula asked.

Harry looked up and the Count was hanging from the ceiling, or rather floating there. Upside down. Smiling. His fangs showing.

"Whoops!" Harry said.

HARRY WOKE UP SUDDENLY, his heart pounding from the terror of that moment in his dream when he discovered the Count had been watching him and Mina make love.

Gads! He thought to himself. *I can't even get away with it in my dreams!*

"Harry? You awake yet?" Mina called from outside his room.

He hurriedly put on his pants and shoes, then a shirt over his bare chest and opened the door.

She stood there like an angel, all dressed in white silks with a pure red rose woven into her hair. "You look terrible, Harry."

"If you had been in my dreams, you would be too." He offered.

She smiled and touched the bare part of his chest gently with a forefinger. "Just make sure those thoughts don't reach father."

He shivered. "Believe me. That's one man I don't want to get angry with me."

"And well you shouldn't, Mister Houdini." Count Dracula said, slipping into the room from beside Mina, where he had been listening.

He wore all brown suede clothing. A suit, tie, and top hat, as well as trousers and shoes.

"You look sharp, Count." Harry complimented him...

"Yes. I do. Don't I?" The Count said with a smile.

Then his smile went away. He jabbed Harry in his chest to make a point. "And I have fine hearing as well. Don't you ever think you can fool around in my house and get away with it, young man!"

Harry swallowed hard.

"I wouldn't dream of it, sir."

The Count eyed Harry a long time. "Perhaps. But anyway, that is not why I have sent Mina to awaken you."

"Isn't it morning?" Harry asked in surprise.

The Count laughed. "I and morning don't walk well together."

Harry gave him a blank stare.

The Count lost his smile. "You will have my full help in rebuilding your magical supplies and equipment. Just tell Mina what you need, and it will be ordered and delivered promptly to you here."

Harry was surprised. "I'm grateful, sir."

The Count started to walk out, and then turned around. "I hope your intentions with my daughter are more honorable than last time."

"They are sir. Much more so."

The Count gave him a scowl.

Harry hurriedly added, "I mean my intentions were always honorable, but I was confused, foolish..."

The Count looked Harry straight in the eyes, his fangs dropping into view. Harry felt very dizzy for a moment. The Count looked away and smiled. "Not just foolish, but an idiot as well."

His fangs retreated... "I will forget what went before; but it will not happen again."

Harry nodded over and over until the Count left the dungeon, laughing all the way.

Mina laughed.

"What's so funny?" Harry demanded. "He threatened my life."

"You look like a bunny caught by a fox."

"No. More like a human caught by a vampire."

She looked hurt.

He hurriedly took her hands and kissed them. "I meant no harm by those words."

She looked up, a grin on her face. "I know, Harry. Now that father's gone for the day, I have something I want to show you."

Harry gave her a blank look. She edged closer and then shoved him back onto his bed.

"Oh my God!" He uttered as she slipped from her pure white dress and walked slowly towards him.

"Oh, dear Harry, God would not do to you what I am about to." She laughed and then shoved him back onto the bed and dropped onto him.

"Before I get my throat ripped out by your father, can you at least tell me where he's going, leaving you alone like this?"

She looked into his eyes. "Hunting."

Then she shut his mouth with hers, shoving herself against him with all her might until they fit like a hand in a glove.

His last thought before he got lost in the bliss was "I wonder what a vampire bite feels like."

Then she bit him.

The Army of the Night

Scar was seated against the mausoleum, his eyes closed, waiting for whatever was supposed to happen, to happen. He opened them once and saw that the Commandant still stood before the uncovered graves and the opened coffins, like a prison guard over his charges.

He grunted. The man was obviously crazy. He was beginning to wonder if he was as well. How could anyone associate with a monster like the Commandant and truly be sane themselves?

He was a man who could crush Scar as easily as he could break an egg with just his fist. That image frightened him, but what was more frightening was that the moon was full and casting its silver ambience directly on the coffins now, giving them an eerie kind of life.

A humming grew in the distance.

He had just been falling back to sleep when he heard it. He opened his eyes and craned his neck to look. The other men gathered close to him for warmth all roused, stretched, and peered about them, not certain where the sound was coming from.

The Commandant raised his metal fist high into the air. "Heil Odin!" He called out.

Scar and his men all jumped to their feet as a silver disc whose bottom was lit up with violet energies burst forth over the treetops and slammed to a stop over the Commandant and the coffins.

The Commandant looked back at Scar and smiled. "Now you will see just how powerful we are!"

Beams of light erupted from the bottom of the saucer and lanced into each of the coffins. The humming sound grew louder and louder.

Scar and his men had to clap hands over their ears to protect their hearing.

70

The sound just kept getting louder and louder, the lights brighter and brighter.

Then Scar and his men lost consciousness and dropped to the ground like flies.

Only the Commandant remained standing.

He spread his arms over the coffins like a god offering blessings.

"Rise!" He commanded.

"Rise and obey me!" He ordered.

The coffins began shaking as if a giant hand were rocking them from side to side.

The Commandant stepped back several paces and continued to watch.

Then one by one, very slowly, emaciated hands clasped the edges of the coffins and slowly, slowly the ghastly heads of mummified corpses began to rise into view, some of them spewing maggots and worms as they rose.

The Commandant began to laugh. Louder and louder. He turned to look at Scar, his eyes more frightening even than the corpses rising from their coffins.

Except he wasn't looking at Scar, his eyes were focused somewhere only he could see.

"I know who you are. And I will find you. I...will...find...you!" The Commandant swore.

Scar could swear that was when he pissed his pants.

The saucer's lights winked out and it shot straight up into the sky and vanished.

Dawn of the Dead

221B looks like the average flat on Baker Street, nothing out of the ordinary. Which makes it more remarkable that this morning would be any different than before for anyone who lived there or happened to be awake.

Constable Marley swung his night stick contentedly as he strode up the sidewalk, whistling a tune to keep himself awake and alert. Nothing much happened on most of his route, but he'd heard that he needed to be extra alert on Baker Street, which was why he took the extra effort to make himself more alert but was failing. He shouldn't have stayed up all night with his friends. He wasn't a young man anymore. At thirty he was pushing it to do those kinds of things like a young kid.

Once he reached the so-called danger zone that was 221B, he stopped whistling and swinging his nightstick. Not because he sensed anything, but because he knew that if anything was likely to happen, it'd probably be here.

He was wrong.

As he crossed the street to reach the front of 221B, he immediately regretted not paying more attention to the alley he had just passed.

Especially once he heard the trampling of many feet in unity. He turned around and gasped.

Struggling towards him, which is the only way he could describe the horror before him were a dozen corpses.

"Blimey!" He swore, a smile lighting his lips. "Are you guys in some kind of party going on? You look terrible. Enough to frighten the socks off a ghost, you are."

But as they got closer, his surprise and humor swiftly turned to abject fear. He could see through the mouths of some of the corpses to the other side.

He crossed himself, counted the number of bodies coming towards him and did the only sane and sensible thing possible at that moment. He ran for his life.

As the sun began to rise on the edge of the city a shadow swooped down towards the horde of the living dead. It swept through them, cutting off one head after another with a wicked long blade. A scimitar whose blade was made of finely honed steel.

The shadow didn't stop until every single body lay still on the street and pavement of the sidewalk.

Once all were down, it swept off rapidly into the sky and vanished, a trail of smoke pluming behind it.

Father Son Conversation

Harry yawned. It had been a long, long night. "Those dreams are really wearing me out," He told himself and then he sat up, absolutely terrified for a moment. "It's not a dream!"

Then he realized who was still in the bed with him.

"Oh, dear God!" He cried out. "I'm a dead man!"

Mina woke, startled by his exclamation. "Harry, what's wrong?"

"Nothing." Count Dracula uttered with a smile as he entered the room, wiping at the long scimitar blade in his hands.

Harry mistook the image immediately and began grabbing for his magic potions.

"Oh, get over yourself, Harry." Count Dracula told him, as he sat down next to the bed, wiping at the tip of the blade.

"Had I wanted you dead; you would never have awoken." The Count explained.

Harry didn't relax. He tensed further.

Mina laughed, got out of bed, slipped back into her clothing, and gave her father a kiss on the cheek. "Father, you're such a scoundrel sometimes. Go easy on him, please."

He gave her a bright smile. "Harry and I are going to have a little talk. That's all."

Mina laughed again. "You'd probably get better results if you put your pin sticker away."

She eyed it uncertainly a moment. "Why isn't there any blood on it?"

The Count smiled. "Let's just say the ones who lost their heads, just couldn't muster up a decent quart."

Harry paled.

Mina laughed again, knowing full well how her father's humor worked. She looked at Harry. "Love you."

Harry was speechless. He made a choking sound that should have been, "Love you," but came out like "lowdy wark."

She laughed again and left up the stairs.

The Count pulled his chair closer to Harry. He looked him straight in the eyes. "What are your intentions with my daughter?"

Harry looked at the tip of the sword which was now only inches from his throat and gulped. "Only the best, Count."

The Count's eyes narrowed. "And that's why you slept with her while I was gone?"

"Actually, she forced me!"

The Count's blade came closer. "After my warning, you still slept with her!"

"Uh, no sir, I mean. Yes. No. I mean, I could hardly do that with you here now, could I? I mean!"

Harry closed his eyes a moment, and then quickly opened them, fearing the Count would mistake what he was doing.

"I mean, I love her. It's what people in love do."

"After marriage." The Count reminded him.

"Mostly." Harry stumbled out the word.

The Count barked with laughter and tossed the sword over his shoulder. It slammed point first into a piece of artwork that hung there, piercing the gentleman's heart that stood in the painting.

"I like a good sense of humor in a man." The Count said. He rose and said, "But if you break her heart again the next time that sword will find your heart! Are we clear?"

"Sir, yes, sir! Perfectly. Like a crystal ball!" Harry agreed vigorously.

The Count sighed, and then sat back down. "Now, on to business."

"Business?"

"Yes. You don't think I was off for a pleasure tour of London at dawn, do you?"

Harry shook his head.

"You must return to Baker Street at once. Your friends will need you there."

Harry jumped from his bed so fast; he startled the Count, who hissed, causing his fangs to shoot out.

"Sorry, sir. Didn't mean to frighten you." Harry quickly apologized, as he began throwing his pants and shirt on.

The Count sighed. "I'm getting too old for this. Maybe I should go back to just sucking blood again."

Harry gave him a frightened look.

The Count smiled. "I'd never dream of taking your blood, Harry. At least not yet." He added ominously.

Harry grabbed his overcoat and fled up the dungeon stairs to the laughter of the Count behind him. The Count was laughing, but he knew the man had been deadly serious. If Harry screwed up his relationship with Mina this time, there'd be no third chance No chance to screw anything at all ever again.

With that thought in the back of his mind he rushed from the dungeon to the light of day, fear for his friends taking over from his own personal fears.

221B Battleground

Watson and Holmes came down the stairs onto the walk quickly as several Constable Wagons, sirens blaring pulled up and Constables rushed out to cordon off both ends of the street.

Inspector Bloodstone exited the last car with his son and joined them.

"Dreadful." Watson muttered at the sight of the headless corpses on the pavement and street.

"Don't worry, Watson."

Watson looked at Holmes questioningly.

"They have been dead for a long time already."

Watson went to the first corpse and kneeled next to it. He touched a shoulder, and it collapsed inwards, throwing up a thick layer of dust into the air. He choked on it a moment, then hurriedly backed away as he stood to get away from the horrid powder.

"They appear to be old corpses," Watson declared. "Quite old, indeed."

The Inspector eyed the heads in various positions all over the place.

"Well, I'm glad of that much, though I imagine this hasn't done much for rent values here." The Inspector joked.

Ms. Hudson exited the flat, stood next to Watson and shuddered. "I wondered what was going on earlier."

Watson and Holmes turned to look at her.

"I've been afraid to talk about this since the incident with Mister Dark, but sometimes I get these visions..."

Watson took her hands in his. "You can tell me anything. You know that."

She smiled into his face, and then it fled, replaced with doubt. "But they are so strange, I'm just not sure if they are real or not."

She paused, and then looked away, "Least not until they actually happen."

"So, tell us, Ms. Hudson, what you saw?" Holmes urged her, his bright eyes fixed on her face.

She looked away again. "I saw myself in this old place. Kind of dark and damp, with lumps of stone in it."

"How were they shaped?" Holmes asked.

"Like..." Her face brightened. "Like tombstones. That's it, it was a graveyard. That explains all the coffins!"

Holmes glanced at Watson, whose own face appeared stricken by the vision. He worried so much about his love and this just added to it.

"Oh, and one more thing, there was this strange man. No..." She faltered a moment, grasping her head as if it might explode. "A very, very tall man, all wrong. He was..."

"A giant?" Holmes finished for her.

"Why, yes," she said, looking at him. "And he had this fist that was strange. Like some kind of metal."

"Go on, Ms. Hudson."

"And then he turned and began laughing. He was looking straight into my eyes. "

She shuddered. "It was like Mister Dark all over again. Those horrible, horrible eyes. He could see me. In my dreams. He could see me. And...And..." She began to panic. "He said he would find me!"

She began to sob.

Watson pulled her close, but she refused his comfort at that moment. "And there was more. I saw this dark shadow fly past my window this morning, even though my eyes were shut. I awoke immediately, but when I realized the light was out, the curtains drawn, I assumed it was still part of my nightmare or whatever it was."

She looked again at the foul remains about them. "And now seeing all this."

She looked at Watson. "Oh, John, I don't want to see these horrible things! These terrible visions. Please make them go away!" She pleaded, breaking the heart of Watson and every man standing there at that moment.

Watson enfolded her in his arms and comforted her, feeling her heart beating heavily against him.

Holmes' lips compressed.

Watson gave him a knowing glance.

JOHN PIRILLO

"Holmes. Watson!" Harry cried out, as he leaped from the back of a noisily braking Tesla cab and joined them.

He stopped when he saw all the corpses. "So that's what he meant."

"Who?" Watson demanded.

"The Count." Holmes answered for Harry.

Harry looked at him. "But how did you know?"

"I would not have, had Ms. Hudson not spoken of her vision prior to your arrival."

Holmes climbed the steps to the flat entrance and peered about several minutes. He found a familiar symbol scratched into the wall. He sighed, and then shook his head as the others joined him. "It would appear that we remove one curse, and another appears."

The Inspector growled. "Your home is no longer safe. We need to get you to a safer place."

"I could never leave here." Ms. Hudson declared, shaking her head.

"Inspector, we need to find that graveyard. Now!"

The Inspector nodded. "I'll have every man on it." He turned to Ms. Hudson and gently touched her arm.

"I swear we'll find that god-awful place and those fiends terrorizing you!" He promised.

Holmes didn't answer; he was on his knees on the street, scraping the feet of one of the corpses, and then into a small vial. He pocketed it, opened another and carefully swabbed the cloth of the cuff of the corpse. He repeated that on several other corpses, and then turned to look at the others who were watching him.

The Mausoleum

"Here, see this." Watson uttered as they came to a stop beside the mausoleum. "Open graves. Twelve of them."

Holmes nodded. "The exact number of corpses we found at Baker Street."

He turned to the Inspector. "I want every one of those coffins dusted for fingerprints."

"On it." The Inspector said, taking the lead and guiding his men to the various coffins. A Forensics Specialist came to the front and the Inspector pointed to all the coffins.

Harry tossed a small portion of magic dust into the air. It began to take shape.

It grew into a giant figure with an outstretched hand.

"Curious." Homes noted.

Watson said, "Harry, is that the actual size of the man who stood there?"

"Give or take a few inches, I'd say so." Harry pointed out.

Watson frowned. "That man's a giant."

Harry sucked on his lower lip and then ventured what he'd been thinking. "I think I've seen this one before."

Holmes turned a curious face on Harry.

Harry looked him in the eyes. "Germany."

Holmes and Watson exchanged looks. Harry said no more, though he looked like he wanted to.

Captain Byrnes almost ran into view, breathing raggedly. "I came as fast as I could. Oh..."

He stopped at first sight of the magical giant that began to dissolve before them all.

"Captain, what do we know of German giants?"

The Captain's eyes narrowed.

"That is sealed information. There is no way you could have found that out."

"Curious," Holmes commented. His face turned to stone. "Captain, you must not hold out on us, lives are at stake!"

"It's a long story." Captain Byrnes replied, his face perspiring heavily.

"Humor me." Holmes urged.

Captain Byrnes nodded. "When I was in Heidelberg several months ago on a special mission..."

Harry's Dungeon

"Quaint." Was the only comment that Holmes could come up with as he and Watson set their luggage down.

Ms. Hudson followed down several moments later and Watson ran to help her with her piece of luggage. She smiled. "Thank you, dear."

He smiled back. "I'm afraid our new accommodations are a bit..."

She gasped when she saw the extent of the dungeon. "Why it's marvelous."

"I was thinking more along the lines of ghastly." Watson added.

She pinched his cheek. "You would, dear." She told him and then began pacing the room.

Mina and Harry stood next to Harry's bed watching.

"What's she doing?" Harry asked.

"I would guess the same thing I would do were I in her shoes. Figuring out where to put things."

Harry groaned.

She patted his cheek gently. "Harry, its war. Sometimes we have to make sacrifices."

"But now we'll have nowhere private." He complained in a whisper.

Holmes smiled. "Don't worry, Harry, we won't take up that much room, will we, Watson?"

Ms. Hudson came up quickly smiling. "Oh Harry, this place is perfect. I'll have it fixed up in no time. Mina, let's talk, shall we? I'm sure you must have as many ideas as I how to make this place more..." She scowled at the dungeon a moment. "Uh, livable."

Mina laughed at the distressed look on Harry's face. "I'd love to. Maybe I can give you a few ideas how to handle where to put Harry's things. He's such a beast when it comes to putting things away." She winked at Harry.

He groaned.

Homes and Harry watched as the two women ascended the dungeon steps, chattering away like a pair of schoolgirls during lunch break.

Watson sat on the edge of Harry's bed and put his head in his hands. "What have we gotten ourselves into?"

Harry sighed. "Heaven only knows," Harry replied.

Holmes smiled. "Oh, cheer up, gentlemen; at least we will have plenty of chances to play chess together. And when Challenger and Conan arrive..."

Harry gave Holmes a distressed look. "Challenger and Conan too?"

"You didn't think we'd leave them in harm's way, did you?" Watson snapped.

Harry sat down as Watson got up.

"I think I hear them now." Watson uttered and headed for the steps up.

Holmes patted Harry on his shoulder. "Don't worry, Harry. We'll sort all this out in the long run."

"It's not the long run I'm worried about, Holmes. It's the short."

Holmes smiled and followed Watson up the stairs.

Harry looked at the huge dungeon space, which very soon would become all too small and sighed.

A tiny black widow dropped on a thread in front of Harry, and he flung a burst of magic at it, incinerating it immediately.

"I'm not in the mood!" He told the crisped spider lying on the floor and then he stomped on it.

Underground Base

Dozens of workers flit about the room, sorting paperwork, cleaning weapons, stacking crates, arranging boxes of ammunition on long tables, where the bullets were passed from one man to the next and then finally loaded into small caliber weapons.

Semi-automatic rifles with bizarre night scopes on them were being racked to the left and shoulder launched rockets with blinking red eye tips were being carefully loaded into crates of straw and covered for shipment.

Scar circulated about the room, observing the activity, and taking notes on a notepad in his right hand. He spoke quietly to one man, who appeared distracted, and the man immediately got back to work, hurriedly placing hand grenades on bandoliers, which when finished, he would hang on a series of racks behind him.

Satisfied with the activities Scar sat down behind Commandant Kepfler's desk, arranged the notes he had been taken and prepared to analyze them. He was interrupted by the sound of the massive door from the labyrinth opening and closing.

He ignored it, continuing to do his work until he heard a familiar tread upon the hard concrete floor. He looked up, saw the Commandant, and replaced his notes in a brown folder marked "Commandant."

Commandant Kepfler hadn't seen Scar at his desk because he was checking out all the activity going on. He hadn't ordered it and it puzzled him and then he saw Scar seated behind his desk. HIS desk!

Before he could bellow the rage, he felt, Scar gave him a warm smile. "I'm glad you could make it, Commandant. We have much to talk about."

"You're at my desk!" The Commandant snarled.

Scar gave the Commandant a patient smile. "Not any longer, it's not."

The Commandant's face paled.

Scar rose.

All about the room the Germans gathered there to work stood up and turned to face the Commandant.

Scar walked around his desk and confronted the giant. He handed him a message.

"Herr Himmler's orders."

The Commandant ripped them up without reading them. He glared into Scar's face. "You betrayed me!"

Scar didn't budge. "Go ahead, kill me if you dare, but you can't kill all of us!"

The Commandant snarled again, turned about, and realized it was true. Everyone had a hand on their weapon and was watching him closely.

He turned back to Scar, who gave him a petulant look.

"I am a loyal servant of the Verboten Party." The Commandant said.

"Good." Scar replied, a look of pleasure and relief on his face. He sat back down behind the Commandant's desk. He folded his arms and leaned forward.

"After the message you received, another came."

"Let me read it." The Commandant insisted.

Scar shook his head. "Impossible."

The Commandant's temper began to show on his face.

"I have to insist!"

Scar shook his head again. "That would be impossible."

"And why is that?" The Commandant demanded, a threatening look on his face.

"Because I am the message." Adolph replied as he strode into view from behind a rack of uniforms he had been examining.

His face was like granite as he approached the two men. His tiny mustache twitched with irritation as he closed in on them.

"Heil Himmler!" Everyone saluted.

The Commandant's face smoldered with anger, but he did nothing as he turned to face Adolph. "Why has Herr Himmler appointed this idiot to take my place?"

Adolph gave the Commandant a look that appeared to be strained at best. "You doubt his integrity, Commandant?"

The Commandant's face paled. "No. It's just that I..."

Adolph didn't hesitate. He strode forth and smacked the Commandant on the side of his face with his cap.

The Commandant stood there shocked as this man so much shorter than him stood before him, glaring into his face with utter contempt and anger.

"You struck me!"

Adolph's face became transfigured with something dark. "You and your sort may be helping us, Commandant. But you do not run the show. Never forget that. This is our world. Ours!" He yelled.

He struck the Commandant again. "Do you understand me, Commandant? Do you understand?"

The Commandant lowered the arms he had been raising and lowered his head. He slowly looked up, and then came to rigid attention. In a voice as cold as ice and wind in a Christmas storm, his eyes hard as steel, he said. "Only too well."

He slowly raised his iron fist.

Everyone tensed, hands reaching for their weapons.

Not lost on the Commandant he shouted, "Heil Odin! Heil Himmler!"

Adolph smiled but didn't salute. Everyone else did. Over and over and over.

War Time Baker Street

Ms. Hudson, Mina, and Harry tended to an antique store in the back of the room, where fresh fish was being slowly fried in a delicate blend of rice wine and sauces made from carrots, apples, and grapes.

"Smells heavenly." Watson commented after his stomach growled like a lion.

Ms. Hudson turned about and gave him a quick peck on the cheek. "It's Harry's recipe."

Watson gave Harry a look of new respect. "I'm impressed."

Harry smiled and dove into a metal container, containing mild cheeses blended in garlic and spearmint. "My father taught me this recipe. It's as old as our family heritage."

He tossed the ingredients on the simmering fish and a wonderful fragrance exploded into the air, causing Watson's stomach to roar again.

Everyone laughed.

Mina gave Harry a smile and he took her loose hand and kissed it. "You were right; this isn't so bad after all."

"Drat it all, Holmes!" Challenger roared on the other side of the massive chamber.

They turned to look where Holmes was setting up the chess board again after having beaten Challenger for the twentieth time.

"How can anyone win twenty times in a row like that?" Challenger roared, but a bit more softly now that he was aware everyone in the chamber was watching him.

Holmes smiled. "Chess is highly logical. You are not, Professor Challenger."

Challenger was about to explode again, but instead sighed and slumped back into his chair. "Very well. I go first this time."

Holmes smiled and waited for the first move.

Conan, who had been stretched out on the special cot like bed that had been brought in by the Count earlier, sat up and yawned. "Is it time to eat yet?

"I would say so." Watson commented, as he and Ms. Hudson hurriedly began setting dishes, silverware and cups on a large round table that had been brought into the room earlier by the Count, who had lifted it as easily as if he were carrying a small chair.

The Count drifted down the stairs, barely floating above them. He touched down on the floor and went to the table. He sat at the far right and placed a napkin in his lap.

Harry set a plate before him. "I don't know what you eat, so forgive me if I make any mistakes."

The Count smiled. "Just remember I don't..."

"...Drink wine," Harry said with a smile.

The Count laughed.

Mina and Ms. Hudson whispered to each other.

"I think Harry and your father are getting along well, don't you, Mina?"

Mina smiled. "I hope so."

Ms. Hudson gave her a worried look. "Is something wrong?"

Mina looked reluctant to speak at first, and then she let it all out in one burst. "I'm pregnant!"

The Count's ears twitched, and he immediately turned around to look at Mina. "You're what?"

Everyone turned to look and listen.

Mina swallowed hard. "Uh."

Harry stood up for her. He stood next to her, took one of her hands and kissed it. "We're going to have a baby."

The Count rose, his fangs extending.

Harry continued but lost his smile. "After we've exchanged our vows."

The Count's fangs retracted, Challenger put away his silver knife, Holmes his silver fork and Watson his pistol.

Tragedy averted yet again, but for how long.

"Dinner is served!" Harry announced.

Everyone got up and came to the stove. Harry, Mina, and Ms. Hudson began serving the fish, a light stew made from potatoes and rice, a boiling pudding with chocolate mixed into a vanilla topping and large slices of freshly baked bread topped with mounds of butter.

They all sat down at the round table and started to eat.

Holmes cleared his throat.

Everyone stopped to look at him.

Harry immediately put his right and left hands on the table. Everyone joined hands.

Holmes lowered his head. "We give thanks for our bountiful meal, our splendid shelter, and our very, very good friends."

He looked up with a smile. "Whom God has granted us the favor of!"

Everyone raised their glasses.

The Count raised his. It was filled with water. "To victory."

"To Victory." Everyone chimed in.

Then the Count gave Harry a withering glance. "And my soon to be son-in-law, long may he live."

Everyone burst into laughter when Harry's face turned as pale as a ghost.

Mina poked her father in the side. "Dad!"

He lost his solemn look and burst into laughter.

Everyone began eating and exchanging pleasant small talk.

A new life had begun for them all. And their friendship was not broken. For it was as hardened as steel in a forge of intense fire. And it would not be easily destroyed, by man or beast!

Times might get more difficult, harder to prevail, but when times get more difficult, the strong rise to the challenge and become stronger!

Holmes rose and clapped his hands.

Everyone turned to look at him.

"Watson." He smiled at his friend, who gave him a nod. He continued, "Had a great idea and one I whole heartedly embrace."

He paused to build tension, then nodded to Watson, who rose, then went to a crate by the stairway. He opened it up while everyone watched expectantly. He lifted something rectangular shaped. He walked to the table and turned about so everyone could see.

"Our new address." Holmes proudly announced.

The wood was a plaque and it had clearly inscribed on it in bold white and gold lettering 221B Baker Street.

A round of laughter pealed about the room and then everyone was silent.

Holmes turned to Professor Challenger who rose and cleared his throat.

"By authority of King Andrew we have been given this round table for a very good reason."

Harry grinned. "I was wondering when you'd get to telling everyone what this piece of wood is."

Challenger grimaced at Harry, and he shut up.

"This is the original round table of King Arthur."

The room was filled with surprise and comments as the gravity of that information sank in. Finally, Challenger sat down.

Holmes rose again.

"My friends, we are at war with a nation guided by darkness. We must always put the higher good before anything else! Anything!"

Silence.

He smiled.

"Today we are no longer just the Brotherhood of Baker Street, but we are also the hope of a nation at war. We are the Knights of a new round table and one that I believe will bring hope in a time of ever-growing anxiety and fear."

Holmes face hardened. "And I promise you this. No stone will remain unturned until we rebuke and remove this evil that has reached our fair lands. We shall pursue it to the ends of the earth if we must. And we will.... we must prevail!"

The Count belched.

Everyone turned to look at him. He held a glass of wine in his hand. He gave them a look of embarrassment. "I do not drink wine."

Harry gave him a scowl. He looked at Harry.

"Well."

Everyone broke into laughter.

Soon everyone had settled down. Watson passed the plaque around for everyone to look at closely.

Holmes looked across at Challenger. "The night is young."

Challenger shook his head. "Not me. I'm tired of losing."

The Count looked at Holmes. "At last, I have a chance to play a worthy partner."

"You're on!" Holmes told him, then got up and secured the chess board and box and brought them to the table.

Ms. Hudson and Watson walked up the stairs from the dungeon into the cool air outside.

He took her hands in his. "Somehow, I feel as if this is all going to end up well."

She leaned into him. Her eyes closed and she happily listened to the beating of his heart, which sped up slowly, but surely.

Yes. It was. It was indeed. She thought to herself.

First Strike

It wasn't the most expedient way to kill as many innocent lives as possible, only the most exceptional. Scar was ruthless and driven to gain more power in the hierarchy of the Verboten Party and because Commandant Kepfler remained a thorn and very real enemy of his position, he had to be bolder than he might otherwise have been.

The Commandant had no idea just how clever he was. He had been tricking quite a few people and some in very high places for years now as he prepared for the final push to victory under Herr Himmler for the Verboten Party.

Even the young and rising star of the party, Adolph Hitler, had taken notice of him. So, he couldn't allow anything or anyone...including and especially the mysterious Commandant Kepfler and all his center world nonsense...to get in the way.

The idea for using lightning as a way of bringing down London wasn't new. The Hollow Man wars of decades before had struck a chord that resonated of the very same diabolical forces at play, but this time it had modern science behind magic, not just sorcery, which Commandant Kepfler and his inner world thugs seemed to be driven by.

He saw them as ancient world. Not modern. Civilization was moving forward from the dark ages of when a few men had great power of mystical sources to many having the power of magic and science combined. It was a brave new world for those willing to take it!

And he didn't give one mark for the Commandant and his people to do anything differently. Yes, they did have advanced technology. But flying discs and guns that fired massive amounts of energy were little more than toys when compared to the use of properly administered terror. He had seen one man in a small country in the Caribbean bring down an entire government by carefully

orchestrated bombs and the use of suicide bombers. He was no less willing to
do the same himself, but in a broader and more massive way. He didn't want
to just bring down London and its hierarchy of overfed nobles and lords and
ladies, but the entire world!

So, it fell upon him to prove to Herr Himmler that he was indeed the best
man to get the job done. And it didn't matter what King Andrews or Churchill,
his son, desired to counter with. He would strike first. Strike hard. And terror
would reign in the hearts of Londoners as surely as if storm clouds had opened
over the heart of the city and drenched it!

And., He smiled to himself. They would never know that without their
help none of it would have been possible. When they finally woke up and
realized how much they'd given away, it would be too late.

"Reveal!" He commanded.

The gigantic screen on the base wall lit up. It had been stolen from an
idea of Nicolas Tesla and Thomas Edison. Right from under their noses. He
had to admire their technical genius. They came up consistently with more
innovations than even the dreaded central earthers, who were capable of some
truly amazing, and often frightening things.

Herr Himmler could never praise them enough. At least that's what he said
in public. Scar wasn't so sure what he said in private. Maybe nothing. Who
knew what the true extent of power they held?

He didn't.

But if Commandant Kepfler were any preview of the capabilities of the
central earthers, then they were more bark than bite, but he also had to admit
that the Commandant's hand was an extraordinary piece of technology equal
to that of anything he had seen developed by the Britains, or the Americans in
their secrecy shrouded lands.

The huge screen measured almost sixty feet wide and twenty in height and
could zoom in and out of details, as well as extruding from the screen in a mock
3D view, which was certainly helpful to some of the underground projects that
were going on around the clock, and around the world.

He smiled. The poor Londoners had no idea how fragile their footing was.
Literally. At any given moment they paced above hidden tunnels and immense
caverns that had been dug out over the last ten years.

Soon, the Britains would be called the Hollow Lands. He smiled at that image. The image of thousands of storm troopers emerging from secret underground bases into the streets of London and every major city of the Britains, firing their powerful weapons and striking into the hearts of all they met a terror and fear unlike any experienced before.

Granted the war was finally coming out into the opening, but the Kaiser had started it many years before, unknown to even the Commandant and his central earther cohorts! And Herr Himmler had inherited his legacy. Notching it even further on the scale of destruction, subversion, and terror.

Scar felt an itching on the mark on his face. He scratched it lightly. He told no one how he had received it, nor would he. Sometimes knowledge could be used as a weapon against someone. If any weapons were to be used, they would be his and his alone.

He would not rule with the brutality of the Commandant. He would show respect where it was due; and reward behavior well done; but he also would brook no failure.

That had been the Commandant's failing; he had allowed Scar to live. He would not make that mistake!

"Activate!" He ordered.

The Techs at the high frequency ultrasound, ultra radiation panels made some adjustments, and all the various connecting communication devices came online. In a matter of moments, the screen lit up with a view of the target.

Big Ben.

It would be the first.

Tiny magical sprites had been summoned and networked about the city, so that this screen could be used properly. It was a brilliant hybridization of magic and science and just the beginning of new weaponry coming online soon.

He remembered from his own research that Big Ben had once been threatened by several home-grown groups who warred with other as the result of magic used by the late Morgana LaFey. They had been dealt quite harshly with in his mind. Had he hired them, he would have merely stripped them of their rank and moved them directly into the battlefield. But the Queen at the time instead chose to teach them a lesson.

He smiled, causing some about him to squirm uneasily, not knowing if he was about to lash out at them or not. He wasn't. He was instead considering what the results of the lesson had become...Verboten!

Morgana LaFey had discovered the magic perpetrated on her prisoners and freed their souls from the bondage made upon them by one Harry Houdini. That man was a continued thorn in the side of everyone who wanted to use magic against the politer rules of Merlin and Arthur.

He sneered, causing more to flinch and fall away about him as he paced the gigantic room. She made friends with the Germanic hordes. Secretly. Not in the open. And a party was formed that wouldn't reach fruition for many centuries. The Verboten Party. Founded on the magics of Morgana LaFey and the technology of the central earthers, a civilization she had sought on an adventure that few knew of. Sought and found!

The Big Ben Caper as that old doctor named Watson called it was no more than a distant memory now, but for him it was fresh. Quite fresh. He read about it over and over, striving to see what he could have done better. For he wanted to use technology when he could. It was easier to hide from the likes of one Harry Houdini, but he also wanted to use both, when possible, Harry Houdini nor not!

But his greatest worry was not Harry Houdini. It was a certain detective. A man who once he latched onto a trail, never let go, just like a bulldog on the chase.

He grimaced at the thought, but knew he had to be careful. What he had done had worked so far. Far greater than any had realized, even Herr Himmler or the Commandant with all his vaunted occult abilities.

He intended to use what had been hidden to his own advantage. He had managed to secret several agents into the libraries of both the King and of the various Royal libraries and museums. Thus, enabling him to subvert all the necessary research to his underground base.

It had taken many months, and during that time, he had fought for the late commander of the base, Commandant Kepfler, but once he had his information and a clear understanding of what the Commander's failings were, he had informed Herr Himmler.

Herr Himmler, in his wisdom had chosen to elevate Scar, much as he had desired to be, making him second only to the golden child, Hitler.

He still remembered that meeting.

Herr Himmler

H err Himmler stroked his mustache in thought.

"So, you believe the Commandant has failed to grasp the significance of what is available, and constricted our efforts to paltry attempts at sabotage, rather than to the larger projects you conceived of which could offer mass destruction, if not victory...to our war efforts?

"I believe so." Scar had told him. He muffled the smile he felt rising from his reception.

Herr Himmler was what many called a scheiss-sniffer. That is, he could tell when someone was not being honest with him. He knew when it reeked of self-appointment and arrogance. So, he had been both blunt and clear in his telling of his experiences. With the Commandant, not hiding a single fact. Yes, some might have put him in a bad light, but Herr Himmler would have found out, and then the Commandant would have seemed like a kitten, compared to the fury of Herr Himmler.

Herr Himmler had turned to his favorite student, Adolph, who stood at attention near a chalk board, writing down notes from the prior conversation. "And you, Adolph?"

Adolph turned his youthful face to peer at Scar. He took his time in gazing at Scar. "I understand your defacement came at great cost?"

Scar instinctively reached for the car on his face, a reminder of that ordeal, but then blushed and hurriedly withdrew his hand. It was a test of his ability to stand up to authority and be strong. "At great cost to the loser, Herr Hitler."

Adolph smiled. It was sincere and warm. He turned to Herr Himmler. "I will check what he has told us, of course, but I feel him to be telling the truth."

Adolph's face then transformed so much that Scar felt terrified for a moment when the man's eyes sought his and without thinking caused him to freeze for a moment as the power of that man's charisma sucked him into the grip of those powerful eyes. "You know the penalty for lying?"

Scar nodded. And that took great effort. Almost as if Hitler were somehow controlling his entire body, willing it to remain non submissive.

Adolph immediately smiled again. He turned to Herr Himmler. "Turn him loose. He can be no worse than the Commandant has been, and he might be better. Meanwhile, I shall check on what he has provided, though my own recent research and sources indicate that they are true."

Herr Himmler smiled. "Trust no source until all sources are revealed."

"Exactly." Adolph replied. He snapped a hand into the air. "Heil Zeus!"

"Heil Zeus!" Both Herr Himmler and Scar had replied, raising their right hands in that ritualistic salute as well.

Adolph had marched from the room, not once looking back.

Herr Himmler had then turned to Scar. "I want you to know that you have my full support but..."

Here, his own face transformed into something truly horrible. "But you must always. Always let me know what you plan before you act. Do not assume because I am replacing one incompetent, I will tolerate another..."

He smiled. "...Even if they are not one of our own!"

Scar had raised his hand in a snap salute. "Heil Zeus!"

Herr Himmler just nodded.

He knew who the real power behind the Verboten Party was. Himself!

Engaged to Destroy

S car spoke loudly, clearing the memories he had fallen into from his mind. He needed to be sharp to carry out the rest of the attack.

"Power up!" He ordered.

All about the base room floor huge generators roared to life. Several men stood at the base of each of them, wands in their hands.

Scar examined the nearest. The two men wore the usual garb of wizards, loose tops and pants that were of woven of a deep velvet black color, with the Verboten Patch on their right arms. The patch had a huge Swastika on it with a lightning bolt through its middle.

The symbol of life and power reversed.

They did not worship God. They worshipped another source. Closer and more malignant.

The wands on all the wizards lit up as one and arcs of energy moved like activated circuits, connecting to the generators in front of them.

A howling wind tore through the base, blowing paperwork into the air into tiny whirlpools of dust and paperwork, and causing many there to huddle in fear as massive bursts of energy were flung from the generators to the tips of the wizard wands.

In a matter of moments, each wand became a massive weapon of great power.

"Strike!" Scar ordered with a shout so he could be heard over the generators.

His voice was amplified by hidden speakers, and the room thundered to the sound of his command: STRIKE!

The Grand Tour

A line of tourists were gathered outside the Tower of Big Ben, waiting for their turn to enter and take the brief tour of the ancient structure. Women, men, and children. Old and young. This was one of the more famous landmarks of London and of the Britains themselves.

A Tour Conductor made his way up the line, accepting tickets, yawning in boredom. He had been doing this for hours now. Soon his fellow Tour Conductor would be leading his lambs...as they called the ones who followed them inside...outside so he could take his own flock inside to give them the grand tour.

The base door opened and the Tour Conductor, his own wife smiled at him and led a happily chatting group of tourists outside, where small tables had been set up to sell them pictures of Big Ben, books written about it and sell refreshments.

He gave her a smile and she returned it. They both missed their children very much. They were a young couple and fortunate enough to have grandparents to watch over their boy and girl during their work time. They would return home to the happy cries of little Michael and Roxanne as they tumbled from their napping beds and ran happily into their arms.

He smiled again, remembering that and then passed his wife with his own tourists. "Ladies and Gentlemen, please make sure that you keep up, as we have a wonderful surprise waiting for you at the top and I wouldn't want you to miss it for anything."

They began ascending the steps that flowed upwards for seemingly miles to some who were not as young as others. "As you know there have been rumors that ghosts are haunting Big Ben."

The crowd behind him all fell silent. They had expected this spiel, but nevertheless began glancing around them nervously.

Suddenly the lights went out.

He stood above them, turning on his Tesla lamp, so they could see well. "No worries, my friends. Just a slight setback. I'm sure we'll be just fine. Our official ghost hunter will be coming any moment now to make sure we are all warded from any evil intent."

The ghost hunger popped from a hidden door and stepped onto the stairwell. He was dressed like a clown.

Small children burst into laughter; others howls of terror. Not everyone liked clowns. But he soon quieted them down when he held up an odd machine in his right hand that made clicking sounds and shot strange lights all over.

"Hush!" He warned.

Everyone dropped to silence.

"I think we're about to see a ghost." The clown whispered conspiratorially.

The clicking became louder and louder.

Even the adults tensed. Their children clutched their hands even more tightly and some slid behind them for protection when the sound began more insistent and louder.

And then the clicking just stopped. Even the lights on the device went out.

The Tesla lamp in the Tour Conductor's hand flickered once and then also blacked out.

The Tour Conductor frowned. That wasn't supposed to happen.

"Henry, what in God's name is going on?" He asked the clown.

"I don't know."

Then the entire room was filled with blazing energies so intense that everyone was instantly blinded. And then they all screamed as pain so intense it felt like they would explode shot through the bodies of every soul on that staircase.

Struck

The Tour Conductor's wife was yawning herself, watching her contented tourist flock happily chatting and purchasing gifts and mementoes of their visit.

Then she felt a sudden shift in air pressure.

"That's odd!" She exclaimed.

Everyone else felt it too. They all looked up and began searching the skies. But that's not where the disturbance was coming from. Not up, but in front of them and in back.

Suddenly, and with no more warning than the hint of something wrong in the air, bursts of light, shaped like lightning, but different, more jagged, more wrong, flooded the entire structure of Big Ben from the ground floor of the building to several feet beyond, snaring people too close to it still and flinging others into the air from the implosion of energies that rippled up and down its structure and inside and out, like some kind of gigantic needle of energy threading the entire structure with blasts of pure energy.

In moments the entire structure of Big Ben lit up like a Christmas tree and was draped in huge arcs of electricity that shot in and out of the structure.

The sound of screams came out the open door at the base. A howling wind picked up and slammed over all the tables, blew away pamphlets, papers, and books and even some of the lighter people standing about.

Those surprised by the flying bodies hurled at them screamed in terror, as they felt themselves lifted by the force of the currents of air playing about the structure and then many were flung against each other, the hard pavement, and some against the structure itself, where they were pinned in horrible curling, tentacles of living energy.

For a moment the Tour Conductor's wife would swear she saw some kind of hideous creature in the formation of energies, its savage eyes and face gloating over the immense destruction it was creating and then she saw through the walls of Big Ben also.

It was horrible! Everyone inside the building was pinned against the walls as lashes of energy fried them to a crisp, sending curls of smoke and fire up and down the stairways and into the chambers and rooms.

In a matter of moments, a bright moment of happiness, calm and excitement had been transformed into one of utter terror.

The image vanished from her sight, and she collapsed to the pavement, along with dozens of others from pain, fear, terror or battering from the intense energies and wind.

Those nearest the structure screamed in pain and horror as their bodies lit up with electrical flames. They ran screaming into the others, who recoiled in horror and fear, knocking others down.

Then as quickly as it had come, the lightning stopped.

When it was through the air became very placid, curls of intense white smoke poured from inside the clock tower and from about the building where the burnt carcasses of tourists still lay, some with hands reaching for rescue, others clenched in pain and distress.

Mothers were huddled with children in fetal positions, their bodies burned crisp, leaving only the outlines of their bodies.

Those who had survived and were still conscious looked up and saw the gigantic hands of the clock were melted and turned into slag that dripped down in huge clumps along the face of the building.

The huge glass face that covered the hands was just melted dropped like icicles down the sides of the building.

And the open door at the base burned fiercely and from inside the tower not a sound could be heard, but a horrible smell, like that of burnt flesh wafted outside.

People turned away and began heaving their guts onto the pavement.

The Tour Conductor's wife rose on an elbow, blinking her eyes in disbelief as she regained consciousness. She slowly staggered to her feet and then stood there frozen in shock, not for a moment believing her eyes and then she collapsed into unconsciousness again, no longer able to bear the knowledge of what she seen and what she now knew to be true: Her husband and scores of others were now no more than smoking ashes!

221B

Holmes and Watson sat at the table playing chess, while Challenger and Conan sat near the window, each reading the London Daily Times. Harry Houdini amused himself and Ms. Hudson by doing small magical tricks that conjured tiny spectral dragons that buzzed in the air, playing tag.

It was a peaceful evening. And rare. So, all were taking advantage of the peace and quiet to enjoy each other and relax.

"Your move, Watson."

Watson stared at the Queen that opposed his own, and his King which had a clean shot from the Bishop of Holmes. He could block it with his knight, but then he would lose his knight. If he moved a pawn, then he would lose his queen.

"Give me a minute, Holmes."

"You've had ten."

Watson glared at Holmes. "This must seem like forever to you."

"Not really. Shall I say the word then?"

"Not yet."

Holmes smiled. Watson knew he was in checkmate but didn't want to admit it yet. He had lost ten times in a row, which was a record for him and his patience, as well as his endurance. He usually didn't last past the first three or four. And he also hadn't eaten a single scone seated next to him. Indeed, a rare moment!

Ms. Hudson looked over. "John, move your queen to guard the rook."

She looked again as Harry conjured another dragon, larger and more brightly colored. It shot lightning bolts from its nostrils.

"How beautiful." She exclaimed.

Watson did as Ms. Hudson told him, fearing the worst. But since he was already in checkmate, what did he have to lose.

Holmes smiled. "I surrender."

"You what!" Watson emoted loudly.

Challenger and Conan glanced over.

Challenger grinned. "Take it while you can, Watson. He doesn't do that every day, you know."

"You mean any day, don't you, Challenger?" Conan quipped.

"Indeed, I do." Smiled an amused Challenger.

"I accept." Watson said, breathing a sigh of relief.

Holmes swept the players into their box, and folded up the chess board and placed it on top the players.

"You gave up easy tonight, Holmes." Watson accused.

"Blame it on our dear Ms. Hudson. She's an astute player." He remarked.

Ms. Hudson laughed. "You mean I pay attention. John is always off somewhere in his head or thinking about his stomach."

Then she saw the full plate of scones still sitting next to him.

"I take that back. Off somewhere in his head," she amended.

Watson scowled at her. She blew him a kiss. He smiled.

She got up. "Thanks Harry, but I better take my man for a walk before he has another fit."

"Another fit!" Watson complained. "I haven't had my first yet."

"Just now, dear." Ms. Hudson remarked. "Come, let's walk."

"I'm not a dog!" Watson complained.

She came over and ruffled his hair teasingly. "No, but you are my grumbly bear. And it's time for grumbly bears to go take their walk." She gave him a meaningful glance and added, "You do know how important these walks are?"

Suddenly, he popped up. "Oh, indeed I do!" He exclaimed, and then quickly added. "A walk is very good for the constitution."

"Oh, so good," she agreed.

He straightened is suit and cleared his throat. "But of course. Where would I be without my evening constitutions?" He asked with a meaningful glance at her.

"Undoubtedly losing more chess games," Conan quipped.

Watson gave him a scowl and descended from the room with Ms. Hudson.

Challenger winked at Conan. "You really know how to get to that man, Conan."

"I should...."

"...I wrote him!" Conan and Challenger said at the same time and then laughed.

Holmes glanced over at them. "Harry, something's wrong."

Harry came over and sat opposite Holmes. "Whatever could it be?"

Holmes squinted at his hands, folded over each other. "I've been having this horrible feeling all night. I don't know why."

Then the room became filled with a light brighter than the sun for some few moments. It was so intense that the rooftops outside were clearly visible for a distance.

Harry and Holmes ran to the window, followed by Challenger and Conan.

In the distance where Big Ben stood were wraps of vivid lightning bolts hurtling away from it and enfolding it.

"Great God in heaven!" Challenger blurted out.

"I think not," Homes said, his eyes narrowing in comprehension.

Aftermath

"I came as quickly as I could," Watson gasped as he ran to join Holmes and Harry on the landing before the great tower of Big Ben.

Dozens of constables had the area roped off, and dozens more were restraining curiosity seekers and those who had lost loved ones from entering the scene of the crime.

Smoke still came from inside the tower and the now open face where the glass had once showed. Slagged metal and glass lay in frozen puddles at the base of the tower.

In one of the slag piles a man's skeletal arm thrust through it into view, clasping a smaller skeleton.

Watson saw it and almost lost his dinner. "My God! That poor soul! And his baby!"

Holmes saw where he looked. "It gets worse, Watson."

Watson hardened himself for what more he would have to see.

Dozens of people lay on stretchers. Victims of the strike, while not burned by the energies, had sustained bruising and other smaller injuries from their panic when the strike had occurred.

Others, much too close to the building when the lightning struck, were now being one by one covered with cloth, put on stretchers, and hauled to waiting ambulances, where they would be taken to the morgue for examination.

Constable Evans patted the back door of an ambulance that was full, and the man inside closed the back door and it drove off. He saw Holmes and Watson and headed for them.

They could see he was quite shaken by the event. His normally red hair was blackened by all the soot and ash still floating about and his lovely uniform was torn in places and smudged with black in numerous spots.

This was true of many of the constables, who had not held back in trying to help those who had fallen and those in shock.

Constable Evans came up, shaking his head. "It's just too much to handle," he swore, shaking his head as if that might help him to somehow make sense of the tragedy. He had been one of the first to arrive. He and his father had been eating at a nearby pub, when Big Ben was struck by lightning.

They had immediately rushed over. What they had seen felt more like something from a battlefield than the world they had just eaten in. It was blackened, worn, impaled by despair and hopelessness, people crying, dying, torn and mangled, wounded and burned in so many ways.

It was boggling to the mind and the soul for both. His father had thrown up his stew and meat. He had not been far behind him in that as well. It had sobered both up in ways they had never imagined possible.

Both knew a war was brewing; maybe even upon them, but the brutal reality of it was beyond comprehension. It was far vaster and crueler than either cared to consider, or ever thought they would have to.

London. The target of mass destruction? Impossible, but here it was. And now.

The Inspector had seen Constable Evans with Holmes and Watson and come to join them. His face somber, his face wet from tears. He had been stricken to his very core by the immensity of the tragedy. He had seen the bodies of small children consumed by the strike and only ashes left. It broke his heart repeatedly to have seen that. His disgust and anger were so immense he thought his heart would break from it.

A woman nearby on a blanket thrust up on an elbow and looked at Holmes. "You must help my son. He's inside the tower."

She collapsed.

"Watson."

Watson nodded and went to her with his black bag. She was moaning in pain, suffering from third degree burns. Watson took out a syringe and a vial and filled the syringe. He injected her with a pain killer and looked at Holmes, then shook his head.

She probably wouldn't make it through the night. She was too old. Too weak.

He began making his way around the victims, stopping next to each one and giving comfort where he could.

Conan was doing the same from the other side where he had started with Challenger's help to administer first aid and relief.

A small child lay all by himself, huddled in a fetal position, holding a small doll to his body. His face was burned badly. Holmes dropped to a knee beside him.

"Daddy?" The small boy asked. He couldn't see who it was. He would never see again.

"Yes, son." Holmes replied softly.

"Mommy had to go away."

"I know." Holmes responded, choking on the words.

The small boy smiled. "She's calling to me. Shall I go with her?"

Holmes put a hand on the child's shoulder. The only part not burned. "She loves you so much."

Watson and the Inspector stood behind Holmes watching, tears coming to their eyes.

"She loves you too, Daddy."

"I know. And I love you as well."

The child reached up his arms for a hug, letting the doll fall away. Holmes took the small child into his arms and held him close. The child went limp.

Holmes stayed in that position a long time, saying nothing, not moving.

Watson finally came over and put a hand on his friend's shoulder. "He's gone, Holmes."

Holmes looked up. "But he will not be forgotten." Holmes swore.

He gently laid the child down on the blanket he had lain on and turned to the others. "None will be forgotten. This I swear!"

His face was filled with so much pain and anger that even the Inspector flinched at the sight. He had never seen this man emotional like that. Ever!

Watson watched Holmes walk away to comfort other victims and turned to the Inspector. "Never ever again let me hear you complain of this man's heart and soul!"

The Inspector stood there, rebuked by the man whom he could hardly stand much of the time, and he said nothing. What could he say?

Holmes was the most intellectual man he had ever known and yet this night he had shown greater compassion than even a saint might display.

He nodded, wiped at tears forming in his own eyes and followed Holmes with his glance. "There will be justice. I swear that to you, Holmes. There will be justice!"

But Holmes did not hear him. He no longer heard a soul. His heart was so clouded with anger that the only thing he saw at that moment was the necessity of solving this crime. At once!

So, he did what he always did best. He began searching for clues.

He took samples of the slagged glass, the metal, and the bodies close to the structure. Samples of the wall, and then he went inside, a handkerchief over his nose so he could breathe and began taking samples of the interior.

Slowly, like a man in a nightmare, he made his way up the stairs, passing over body after burnt body. Like a man almost asleep, he forced himself to continue, his body wanting to rebel and run back down, fleeing from this nightmare of pain and anguish, and yet steeling it to his purpose.

He must know the truth!

Clues

Holmes and Harry combed through the ashes strewn up and down the stairs of the interior of the Big Ben, while Challenger and Conan did the lower area. Constable Evans worked the top levels with a squad of other constables, overlooked by the Inspector, who glowered at the heaps of ashes about the room, that once were men, women, and children.

Holmes eyed Harry. "This is not an ordinary fire. People burned. Glass burned. Metal burned, but the rest of the structure is intact as if the heat and flames never touched it at all."

"Magic." Harry said, the one word and simply without even thinking about it.

Holmes shook his head. "What kind of magic could do this, Harry?"

Harry shook his head. "Our world is no longer just technology, Holmes; it is a blend of both technology and magic."

"Then you believe this to be a form of hybrid magic?"

Harry looked into Holmes eyes. "And you do not?"

Holmes didn't reply. He already knew the answer.

Harry nodded. He held up a hand in which a ball of light played. He held it towards the ashes, and nothing happened, but when he held it upwards, it grew brighter.

"Whatever the magic, hybrid or pure, it has a source." Harry explained, as he hurriedly ascended the stairs, followed by Holmes.

They tried not to step into the remains of the people struck down by the holocaust of energies, but it was impossible, there were so many.

Once Holmes stopped. He could see the outline of a child's hand and the remains of a Teddy Bear. His eyes hardened in anger when he saw it, but he forced himself to hurry up after Harry. He had already passed it once before, but it furthered his resolve to solve this case upon witnessing it yet again.

Harry entered the top floor where the gears of the great clock had turned at one time and then stopped. Holmes watched as he slowly moved about the room.

Every constable froze in their positions. They had been dutifully searching for clues as well, but nothing had been found except the remaining ashes of the victims and some burnt clothing or personal items.

"What are you sensing, Harry?" The Inspector demanded before Holmes could speak. He had been guiding the search for clues.

"Shhh." Harry warned.

The Inspector fell back alongside his son, who put a hand on his father's shoulder. "Be patient, father, I'm sure Harry will tell us when the time is right."

Holmes nodded to them and followed Harry as he ascended to the top floor of the gear room. He finally stopped when he reached the main axle of the clock which stuck out where the glass face had once been. Its tip was melted and formed a long drip of metal, which fell down the side of the tower.

Harry looked down, then back at Holmes. "It's incredible. Look!"

Holmes looked at Harry's hand where the light floated. It was so bright he could see through the bones through Harry's skin.

"What does it mean?"

"It means?" Harry asked, shaking his head.

He turned in a slow circle and then as the light dimmed, he went back to his original position.

"It means that I know where the lightning strike came from." He said with a grim smile.

"Where?" Holmes demanded, his eyes dark with anger and the need to do something. Now!

The Underground Base

S car watched a giant image, along with all the others, of the smoking tower of Big Ben. He had a smile of triumph on his face.

Suddenly, everyone broke into applause.

All except the Commandant who was seated near his old desk, his eyes closed, as if asleep.

Scar glowed in the warmth of his triumph. But not for long.

The Commandant suddenly jumped up. His eyes popped open.

"THEY KNOW!" He shouted.

Retaliation and Destruction

Sirens blare loudly, causing scores and scores of windows to open in the night as police wagons spin around corners, accelerate and make their way to their destination.

In the lead car driven by the Constable Evans, Harry and Holmes watch attentively as streets flash by and buildings.

Harry has the light in his palm. It grows brighter.

"Left, Constable!"

The Constable jumps on the accelerator and whips into the turn at full speed, causing the wagon to spin two of its wheels for several moments as they lift from the pavement.

"Right!" Harry hollers.

Constable Evans without questioning swings the car right.

"Left again." Harry commands.

A gang of muggers out to break into a jewelry store this night are suddenly startled by dozens of police wagons heading their way. They make a run for it, but the cars just keep coming. Then they realize that the constables are not stopping. They stop running; gasping for air and give each other confused looks.

Then a second string of constable cars swing into view, dozens more following them. The gang high-tailed it down the nearest alley as the new cars swept past with blaring sirens and flashing lights.

As Constable Evans makes one last fast turn the road opens, revealing the outskirts of London, where great field and meadows extend, but before that a large cemetery that stretches for miles.

"Stop!" Orders Harry.

Constable Evans slams on the brakes and the vehicle goes into a tailspin, whipping around until it's facing the oncoming police cars behind it.

It's a mad house for a moment as they all slam on brakes, swerving right and left to avoid slamming into each other.

Then Holmes and Harry are out the door and sprinting into the graveyard. Constable Evans reaches into his glove compartment and pulls out a revolver. He checks it quickly, and then leaps out to follow his friends.

Behind them Watson, Conan and Challenger leap from another vehicle and follow at a run. They all have weapons out, except for Conan, who has only his brown medical bag.

In moments dozens of constables, armed with weapons follow them.

More and more police wagons continue to arrive and disgorge constables.

Harry slows as they pass through the graveyard. "The light is fluctuating."

"Why?" Holmes demands.

Watson, Challenger, and Conan catch up, panting for air. The Inspector is not far behind.

Dozens of constables come running with weapons drawn.

"Where?" The Inspector demands.

Harry looks at all the expectant faces, and then holds the light up as an idea pops into his head. The light grows dimmer the higher he holds it.

He looks puzzled a moment and then drops to a knee on the moist cemetery sod. He lowers the light, and it begins to flare into life as brightly as ever and brighter still as he touches the ground with his hand and aims it towards an old mausoleum with a cracked door.

Harry extinguishes the light. He rises.

Holmes and Harry exchange a look.

Holmes turned to his friends. "Stay here. Make sure no one else tries to follow us or leave!"

Then he and Harry, followed by the others run for the mausoleum. The Inspector kicks the door once on its lock and its shatters away, allowing the door to be heaved aside.

They enter, igniting Tesla lamps as they do so. An opening is revealed in the base of the mausoleum. Wide enough for two at a time to descend.

The Inspector raises his own weapon and is the first down the stairs, followed by the Constable, Holmes, and Harry.

Behind them a long string of constables follow.

Retreat

The huge door that goes into the underground base is shut with a loud clanging sound that reverberates throughout the huge chamber.

Men and women scramble to get everything packed and placed on carts, which are immediately towed off by other men and women down an emergency exit, where they stow the files and equipment in the back of a small train's cargo car. There are two more, which are hooked to a powerful steam engine miniature train. Ahead of the train are tracks which move off into a tunnel, which is pitch black.

The cargo car is filled and the next is opened and immediately men and women began packing it with supplies and crates as well.

Scar watches from beside the train. He nods to the Conductor. "Get this out of here."

The train chugs off, pulling the weight of its cargo, slowly at first and then gaining speed.

Scar turned to look at the huge base which he is now forced to abandon. Commandant Kepfler watches him like a savage hawk ready to tear into him, his eyes saying more than his lips ever could.

Scar scowls at him then nods to the giant. He moves forward and helps a dozen men to shut off the train opening with a huge door that slams into place, hiding the tracks.

Other men hurriedly place boards over the remaining tracks to disguise them.

Scar waited until his people were gathered before the last exit. "No one must be caught! Heil Zeus!"

"Heil Zeus!" They all responded and fled down the second tunnel for safety.

Scar turned to watch as several men completed the wiring of detonators to the gigantic generators.

He turned to Scar. "They will open this; even as they will open the other, but we will be far enough away it won't matter."

"With luck they won't figure it out until it's too late."

Both men were equally concerned. Something had gone wrong with their protections and neither knew what or why? It was both puzzling and confounding, as it was a major setback to the sabotage work they had begun.

They were forced to leave behind the lightning generators, but they would be blown up shortly after they exited by a remote detonator.

The entrance door was struck hard.

Silence!

Scar and the Commandant looked at each other.

Entrance

"**B**ack! Get back!" Harry ordered.

He flung his entire pouch of magic powder at the huge door closing them off from the underground base, muttering incantations as he did so.

The bag erupted in magical fires and stuck to the door. The fire quickly spread the length and breadth of the door, consuming its thick metal with a furious hunger that seemed more alive than inanimate. For a moment the fire appeared to be a gigantic mouth made of living fire then it vanished, and the fire. The huge door began to bubble and swirl, like a cauldron of boiling oil.

Harry looked at Holmes and the others. "Run!"

They all ran several dozen yards back.

Battle for Nothing

The huge door closing off the base from the outside world exploded outwards and had there been even one person left there, they would have been struck by it, but there were none.

The door rolled across the empty vastness of the chamber, and slammed into one of the generators, which exploded, sending showers of electrical sparks everywhere. A terrible fire began which rapidly spread tongues of hungry flame about the base.

The Inspector, Constable Evans, Holmes, and Harry rushed inside. They were soon joined by dozens of constables who spread out to search the area.

Harry was the first to comment on the generators. "The source of the attack."

"What are they?" The Inspector demanded.

"A hybrid generator." Harry replied. "Stolen from Tesla and Edison no doubt."

Upon Holmes look Harry added, "I saw their plans. Exactly the same."

Holmes grimaced. "It would appear that our saboteurs have a deeper reach into our strengths that we at first thought."

"I'm of a like mind, Holmes." Harry told him. "And it worries me a lot."

"Why?"

"Because they also took that terrible machine the two were working on, remember?" Harry reminded Holmes.

"The power supply that could annihilate an entire city?"

"That one," Harry replied grimly. "Once they build that they won't need tunnels anymore or hidden chambers."

"They'll just be able to blow London off the map," Holmes said.

Holmes didn't say more, instead he ran swiftly through the chamber, searching for clues. "This way!" He cried out and ran for a series of high shelving. He quickly began moving them aside with the help of several constables to reveal the other huge door.

"Another one!" Harry spat out in disgust. "I'm out of ways to deal with this one."

Then Harry's drained of color. "God no!" He exclaimed as he looked suddenly to his right. He held out the light on his palm and it almost flared back to life.

"What is it, Harry?"

"There's something actively giving off magic here. It's big. Really big."

Then they both saw the blinking light on the remaining generator. They also saw the stacks of munitions laid up next to it.

Holmes and Harry turned about and shouted at the same time. "GET OUT!"

They took off as fast as they could for the way they had come in. Everyone sprinted for the exit behind them, not knowing why they had to run, but also not wanting to wait and find out.

Harry found himself falling behind the others. He had hurt himself somewhat earlier that day at Big Ben. He hadn't told anyone. He knew then he should have.

As he slowed to ease the pain, he didn't notice the rod sticking out to his right and struck hard against it, tearing his flesh. He spun about and landed on a discarded file drawer and fell to the floor, slamming his head into the hard pavement. He lost consciousness.

No one noticed in the rush for safety. They were too far ahead now and too filled with fear to hear anything.

The detonator on the last generator ticked down to zero as something dark hurtled into the chamber.

Graveyard of the Forgotten

Holmes and everyone else poured out the opening they had found and raced for the nearby street. They had gotten about halfway there when the graveyard erupted in a huge ball of flames, flinging many of them into the air, consuming others.

The Inspector struck the ground near Holmes. He rolled over, his eyes wide with terror. "Son!" He hollered.

A hand gripped him from behind.

He turned around. It was Constable Evans, his face streaked with dirt and mud.

The Inspector enveloped him in a huge bear hug.

Challenger, Conan, and Watson spread out among the wounded, helping them to their feet and giving aid where needed.

Holmes stood up; a bit staggered by the intensity of the explosion yet. He felt his forehead. It was wet. He looked at his hand. Blood.

Watson came up, his face dark with anger. "The bastards got away again, didn't they?"

"Yes." Holmes replied, his own anger barely restrained.

"You've been hurt!" Watson exclaimed.

Holmes gave him a thin smile. "Only my pride, Watson."

Watson gave him an appraising look.

"Where's Harry?"

Holmes then realized that Harry was nowhere to be seen. They both turned about, searching for him.

Then they both realized at the same time why he was missing.

Looks of horror spawned on their faces.

Elevation

Harry awoke to consciousness on top a building's rooftop. A dark faced man's face peered into his own. "Harry."

"What?"

Count Dracula sat down on the rooftop next to him and gathered his long legs together beneath his chin and stared at Harry thoughtfully. "You didn't think I would let my daughter's future husband just die, did you?"

Harry sat up, rubbed his head, and groaned. "It feels like a goose egg."

"It looks like one too," The Count confirmed with a smile.

He rose and gave Harry a hand up. "I could fly you home?"

Harry shook his head. "I've got to tell Holmes what I saw before the explosion."

"What did you see?" The Count asked.

Harry told him.

The Count's smile vanished.

The New 221B

Holmes paced the floor of the sitting room almost frantically, while Conan, Challenger, Watson, and Ms. Hudson looked on.

No one spoke.

They were in mourning.

Mina sat in a corner on Harry's bed, sobbing. She wouldn't let anyone near her. Or touch her. They had all tried. Unsuccessfully.

"I don't like it one bit," Challenger growled.

Watson nodded. "Not even the Count is here. Maybe he could help her."

"I rather doubt even he could reach her now," Conan chipped in.

Challenger shook his head. "I can't believe that Harry's gone."

Ms. Hudson wiped at the tears in her eyes. "He was so kind and generous."

Holmes stopped. "It just doesn't make any sense."

He turned to look at his friends. "He was right behind us."

No one said anything. What could they? Harry had been left behind.

Holmes felt it more heavily than the others. He should have noticed when Harry hadn't been with them at once. But he was so hell bent on bringing the people to justice that it had clouded his logic.

"It's our fault," Challenger said.

"No, it's mine," Holmes said with a heavy heart. "Harry and I were side by side. I lost track of him, but I was too lost in my anger to notice."

Watson rose and put a hand on his friend. "Holmes, you can't blame yourself. What could you have done anyway? If you had stopped, you'd both be dead now."

Challenger and Conan nodded in agreement.

Challenger sighed. "Death is never a friend, Holmes. Never. It picks whom it wants, and none have the say of its when or why."

"I'm so sorry I ever got mad at him," Watson muttered. He smiled. "He was funny sometimes."

"I as well," Challenger agreed.

Conan shook his head. "He never bothered me."

They all glared at him.

Ms. Hudson got up, still wiping at her eyes and went to Mina. This time Mina threw her arms around Ms. Hudson, and she sat next to her comforting her.

"Well, least that's better," Watson pointed out.

Holmes shook his head. "Nothing's better. We've lost too many. And now Harry. This is intolerable!"

"I agree." Harry said as he descended into the large, revamped dungeon that was now the home of Baker Street and its friends.

"Harry!" Mina cried out, and leaped from his bed and ran to him. She grabbed him so hard about his neck that everyone could hear it pop.

He gave her a kiss, and then pulled her free. "Rumors of my death..."

She put a finger to his lips. "No joking. This is serious."

In moments he was surrounded by his friends all pounding him on the back, hugging him and smiling.

Holmes did not.

When everything had finally settled down, he gave Harry a piercing look. "You know more."

"How can you tell that, Holmes?"

"First, you did not tell us how you were saved. I can't imagine for a moment; you would ever let such a thing go by without bragging about it. Second, I can only conclude that you have already told the secret to someone else, and they didn't want me to see their face because I knew them. Mina's father, of course."

Harry nodded. "That's correct. He saved me from the explosion, though I have no memories of how."

"Three. Your magic is undetectable."

"Yes. That's true."

"And yet it was," Holmes added. "Detectable."

"Which implies someone knew," Harry answered, his eyes widening.

"Four, which means someone close to his Majesty, is in on this," Sherlock continued.

"Yes. And I know who," Harry revealed with a grin that brought smiles to everyone's face.

"Then who, for God's sake, Harry? You're killing me with all this suspense," Watson blasted out.

Holmes smiled. "He can't tell you who, because it wasn't anyone else but himself, wasn't it, Harry?"

Harry lost his look of complacency and sank onto his bed. He put his head in his hands. "All those people dead because of me and my damned arrogance."

Mina sat next to him. "Harry, you can't take the blame for that lightning strike. It was the Verboten Party, not you who did that."

"That's true." He looked up and took her hands.

"But if not for me, they could never have struck with such force."

Holmes agreed. "Yes, but not directly, Harry. Their ruse with the buzz bomb dragons was not to destroy us, though I'm sure that would have been a nice bonus for them."

Harry stood up, excited and grinning from ear to ear. "It was so they could still all my magic, my books, my plans, my inventions..." He stopped for a moment, gasping for air. "Do you know what this means, Holmes?"

"Yes, I do," Holmes replied, his eyes glinting with malice. Not towards Harry but to the one he know knew was responsible.

"Harry would never have betrayed our country, our fellow countrymen," Mina insisted.

Count Dracula stepped into the room, stepping onto the hard floor as lightly as a feather. He flipped his black cape over his right shoulder and then spoke once he had everyone's attention. "No, he would never have intentionally done so, which is the only reason why he is alive today instead of me leaving him to die in that holocaust."

Holmes turned to eye the Count. "Captain Byrnes."

The Count didn't flinch beneath the stare of the Holmes. "I believe so."

Watson was shaken to his very soul. "But how could a man like that betray his friends and country?"

"Easily." Holmes replied with the hint of a smile. "If this were not his country."

"But he's as British as all of us," Harry cried out. "Well, almost all of us," he said, eyeing Count Dracula, who eyed him back, but baring his fangs.

Scotland Yard

The Inspector stood in his office like a statue watching his people go about their business. One constable sorting through the latest arrests. Another helping with fingerprints. Another chatting softly with a mother and son seeking their lost father. His Staff Sergeant busily supplying everyone with coffee and bread to eat to help them make it through the long night.

So much had happened. He had lost ten of his good men in the explosion. At least another dozen were severely burned or wounded by the debris of it.

His son was alive, but he also suffered cuts on his back and neck from flying debris.

He was the only one without cuts or burns. He was sore as hell from the tumble, but otherwise fine. He would gladly have exchanged an arm or a leg to bring back the men who died. He knew their families, their wives, their sons, and daughters. Their mothers and fathers. He would make sure that he spoke to each one of them, to somehow help them understand that the lives lost had meaning.

He always managed to do so, while himself always feeling hollowed out afterwards from his own lack of conviction in the lies he told.

He sighed, pocketed his hands, and turned his back on the outside.

He faced instead Captain Byrnes, who sat at the opposite end of his desk, sipping at tea.

"Will Holmes be here soon?"

The Inspector nodded. "Soon enough. I imagine he's still quite busy from the other night."

"I would too," the Captain agreed. "I just wish I could have been in on the fight as well."

"Well, we all have our jobs to do, don't we, Captain?"

Before Captain Byrnes could reply Watson stepped into the office.

"Inspector." Watson greeted.

The Inspector turned and Watson stood in the entrance to his office.

"Come. Come in, Watson. Where's Holmes?"

"He'll be here shortly. He's waiting for someone."

Watson took a seat to the right of Captain Byrnes. "Captain."

"Watson."

"Some tea, Watson?" The Inspector asked, gesturing to a fresh pot on his table and some extra cups.

Watson shook his head and when he saw Holmes and Harry approaching, he sat down on the left of the Captain.

A moment later Harry and Holmes entered. Holmes sat down on the right side of the Captain. Harry stood at the entrance without entering all the way.

"Captain." Holmes greeted.

The Captain nodded.

"I guess we can proceed now," the Inspector remarked as he sat down behind his desk.

He opened one drawer but didn't go into it. He eyed its contents thoughtfully, and then looked at the Captain. "It seems we had a bit more on our plate the other night than just the Verboten Party."

"How's that, Inspector?" The Captain asked, surprised at this turn of conversation.

"Holmes."

Holmes gave the Captain a thin smile as he faced him. "As you know our operation was done in the utmost secrecy."

"But of course," the Captain responded with a nod. "His Majesty, Prince Churchill would insist on that."

"Yes. He would," Holmes agreed.

The Captain gave Holmes an expectant look.

Holmes took a small pad from his inner coat pocket and set it before him. "I've gathered a few of my thoughts here and wondered if you could help me clarify them."

Holmes smiled at the Captain. "You've known the Prince far longer than any of us here."

"Yes. That's true. We grew up together. Went to the same military academy."

"Phillips, I believe?"

"Yes. It was instituted by the late Queen Mary of Scots."

Holmes glanced at Watson, who merely stared straight ahead, though his right hand was near his coat pocket as if holding his heart in. He tapped his fingers there lightly, as if considering the conversation. Something in his expression had hardened, as it also did on Holmes face, but was lost on the Captain, who continued to sip at his tea.

"Is there any chance he might have spoken to anyone outside of our circle?" Holmes inquired in a friendly manner, his eyes on his notes.

The Captain's eyes narrowed in thought. "No. He's pretty close-mouthed when a big operation is going down."

"Yes. I believe he would be," Holmes agreed.

"So, what are your questions that I can help you with?" The Captain inquired politely.

Holmes glanced at his pad. He held it up so the Captain could see it well. "Do you know this man?"

The Captain looked closely at the drawing, which showed a man with a scar on his face. He frowned. "Looks like the man we've been dogging for so long now."

"Yes. It is him," Holmes confirmed. "We have done some research at the Thames Ironworks where he worked. His name is Scar."

"Unusual name but considering the lowly nature of many that work there, maybe not," Captain Byrnes admitted.

Holmes and Watson exchanged another quick glance, again not noticed by the Captain, but noted by everyone else, who tensed.

"And do you notice any outstanding facial characteristics about him?"

"The scar," the Captain replied at once.

"Yes. A rather ugly one, wouldn't you say?" Holmes replied.

"Yes. Must have been a very handsome fellow at one time, I imagine."

Holmes smiled. "Now, tell me who this is...that is, if you recognize this face, Captain."

Holmes showed another page on his pad.

The Captain gave it a look and then a questioning one to Holmes. "I should recognize it, sir. Because it's my own!"

"Yes. Very correct, Captain."

Holmes took the pad from the Captain and set it on the Inspector's desk. He began to draw a line on the face. Next, he altered the pattern of the hair and its color.

"What's going on, Holmes?" The Captain demanded, suddenly growing wary of the proceedings, noticing that everyone was watching him intently.

"Nothing remarkable, I assure you, Captain," Holmes replied.

Holmes finished the mark he had been drawing on the Captain's face. Ripped it from the pad and laid it on the table. He then did the same of the man with the scar on his face.

The Captain looked at them and stiffened.

"Notice any similarities, Captain?"

The Captain jumped to his feet.

The Inspector plucked a revolver from his drawer. Watson withdrew one from his coat and Holmes one from his own.

Harry stood in the doorway, a ball of hot flames leaping into life on his right palm.

"What's the meaning of this?" The Captain demanded; his face flushed with anger.

Holmes rose slowly, but his gun remained unwavering on the Captain's chest.

"I am about to reveal the identity of our traitor," Holmes replied.

Holmes took the right ear of the Captain and tugged at it. In a moment a slab of face fell away, revealing the same scar as that of Scar.

Holmes swiped at the Captain's hair, and it flew off revealing that of Scar's.

"You've sealed your own death, Holmes!" The Captain cursed at him.

"I think it more likely; you have sealed your own. Inspector?"

The Inspector rose and then looked out the door by Harry. He put a thumb to his lips and blew a whistle. His son and about a dozen Constables rushed to the room. He stepped aside and they surrounded the Captain.

"Captain Byrnes, in the name of Prince Churchill and the Good King Andrew, I hereby place you under arrest for high treason against the lands of the Britains."

"You'll never prove that" the Captain replied disdainfully. "I have friends in high places who won't take a liking to this accusation."

"I also warrant you for arrest for the deliberate act of mass terrorism and destruction, which has resulted in the innocent deaths of over a hundred and twenty civilians and..." He gave the Captain a look that caused him to back up. "...My men!"

The Captain threw off his jacket, revealing the Verboten Party swastika on his right arm. He straightened up, gaining several inches of height.

He spoke, but no longer in crisp English, but with an obvious German accent.

"You have won this battle, Holmes. But you have not yet won the war!" He warned with scorn in a very German sounding accent.

Holmes stepped closer, so his weapon was poking Scar directly in the chest. "Perhaps a bullet in your heart would convince you otherwise?"

Scar paled.

"I thought not," Holmes answered to him. He put his gun away and went to the door. "Watson."

Watson put his weapon away and followed Holmes to the door. He turned back to speak to the Captain. "If I were you, I would pray to whatever god you worship to save your soul, for I fear nothing less will save you from the wrath of the King."

"I will not stay in a dungeon cell for long," Scar hissed at him.

Holmes laughed. "No. You won't. Because if you escape, I will hunt you down like the dog you are and shoot you dead."

Holmes turned and left.

Watson followed him out.

The Inspector nodded and his constables marched Scar from the room.

The Inspector turned to his son. "I fear he is not the only traitor to our fair lands."

Constable Evans said nothing. He believed no differently.

221B

Holmes and Watson sat opposite each other playing Chess.

Conan and Challenger sat near the window chatting with Ms. Hudson, who was showing them her latest knitting, a cute towel with a symbol of the Britains upon it.

Harry stood near the door, holding Mina's hand.

"All's well that ends well," he told her.

She snuggled against him. "I fear that will not be the case this time."

He looked at her.

She sighed. "Father tells me there is a gathering force outside the lands."

"Gathering force?"

"Yes. As you know he heads the Council of Vampires and they have been gathering rumors of a vast movement of troops upon our lands."

"From where?"

"The Dark Lands."

Harry grimaced. "So, they intend to fight us not only with superior technology but magic and..."

"Demons," Mina finished for him.

Harry's eyes widened. "The Hollow Man is back."

"I'm afraid so, Harry. Big time."

Challenger scowled. "We beat those zombie bastards back once; we'll do it again!"

"Here, here, Challenger!" Conan cheered him on.

Holmes looked up and smiled at them. "Mina, let us not dwell on what may or may not be, but instead be grateful for what is."

She smiled back at him and then leaned back into Harry once more, who whispered into her right ear, "He's right, you know."

"For a man with a genius mind, he is awfully practical sometimes," Mina agreed, the hint of laughter in her voice.

"Unlike someone we know, huh Harry?" Challenger joked, slapping Harry on his back.

Harry laughed, gave Challenger a scowl, but then nibbled on Mina's right ear lobe.

"Stop that!" She laughed.

"Never!" He told her.

Their eyes met and locked. She brushed her lips against his and he kissed her, gently, but deeply.

Ms. Hudson smiled when she saw it and glanced over at Watson, who sat oblivious to the romancing going on as he pondered how to save his neck in Chess and not lose again.

Challenger and Conan exchanged smiles.

Challenger said, "All's well does not always end well, does it Conan?"

"No, but sometimes it just ends," He said with a smile.

"About that new play by William," Conan inquired of Challenger. "Do you think it's better named Juliet and Romeo, or Romeo and Juliet?"

Ms. Hudson interrupted them. "Oh, I think Juliet and Romeo sounds more modern, more romantic, don't you?"

They laughed.

Holmes sat there waiting for Watson and he felt a great sense of calm descending upon him. He had brought justice to the man behind the horrid terrorist act, and even though the rest of them had escaped, he had confidence he would find their new hideaway and once and for end their appalling plot against the lands and their people.

"Checkmate, Holmes," Watson declared.

Holmes looked at the board and smiled. "Watson, you did it again. And without the good Ms. Hudson's help either. You never fail to surprise me."

Watson beamed with pride. He stood up and took a bow. He turned to his other friends. "I have finally beaten Holmes at chess."

He glared at Ms. Hudson. "And without help!"

She laughed but rose and applauded him. The others did so as well.

Holmes watched Watson with fondness and for just a moment, flashed back to a similar time with his original Watson, when he had let him win. He almost laughed, but Watson might have taken that the wrong way.

Instead, he just bathed in the glow of the warmth that his many good friends felt towards each other and the knowledge that all wars must come to an end. Sooner or later. And no matter what the course of their journey might travel, they would have traveled well and in good company.

He sighed inwardly. He was truly blessed.

Get a Free Book from me.

Learn more about my Sherlock Holmes in the back of this book in the glossary. It will help you to understand the new world I have placed Sherlock Holmes within and those he deals with.

I describe most of my characters and the world the new Sherlock Holmes solves his cases.

Grab a free Sherlock Holmes book on me![1]

Author's Note

I've always had a great love for mystery and adventure. Starting with Agatha Christie's The Bat and ranging to Edgar Rice Burroughs Tarzan of the Apes and Jules Verne's Journey to the Center of the Earth.

It was only a short step between those three writers to run into Sir Arthur Conan Doyle and his wonderful Professor Challenger adventures.

I first read Sir Arthur Conan Doyle's wonderful spread of detective stories when I was still a child. I didn't own books, so I read them at the public library, or my school library. There was no Internet of Things, no Internet at all at the time. I was very into books as a child, always a loner of sorts. Even though I loved people, I was somehow always more in love with books. Call me bookworm then. Now bookworm writer. Maybe.

I went through the entire adult library in my hometown as a child, reading everything from fiction to non-fiction, science fiction to fantasy, and classic literature to modern. It didn't matter. It was words on paper. I loved the smell of books. Still do, even though I cater to electronic books currently.

This is all a back-story of sorts to give you an idea of why my Sherlock Holmes while based somewhat on the canon of Doyle, is nevertheless much more than that. What would be the point of repeating what's already been done?

No, rather I saw this writing experience as an opportunity to allow my imagination to romp in his playground but take elements from other famous authors and stories I've loved over the years.

There are copyright issues when it comes to living authors, so even though I'd love to play in their yards too, that is forbidden territory. So, I have contented myself to take my love of classic literature...Doyle, Verne, Wells,

Dumas, Shakespeare and pour them into a mutual melting pot. Kind of a United States of Literature, so to speak.

Whereas the Sherlock Holmes of Sir Arthur Conan Doyle functions out of London, England in the Victorian period; mine exists in a parallel world where all the authors who have ever lived and all their characters are alive at the same time.

Therefore, if you see me including Houdini and Sherlock together, Challenger and Conan Doyle, it makes more sense if they were alive in that world and not this one.

As a person with a strong scientific background...I wrote a treatise on reaching other dimensions (parallel worlds) as an 8th grader, which my Physics teacher was knocked out about...I believe quite strongly in an unlimited universe, where an infinite number of parallel ones/dimensions exist at the same time.

When I was in India, I found that some there adhere to the belief that everything that man can do or imagine exists in a vast cosmic tapestry so that we do not so much physically exist, as mentally/spiritually move through that infinite tapestry, each choice we make...right or wrong...creating a branching point that we must follow, even though there were already an infinite number of other ones. Remarkably close to the parallel world/alternate dimension approach that many scientists are now coming to accept as a reality.

When I was a kid, the scientists barely believed in 4 dimensions...length, breadth, height, and time. Now as an adult there is talk of at least 9 known dimensions.

But getting back to my stories, what makes them relevant and different is that I can populate them with any science, any character, any famous figure, writer, artist, or whatever and they all fit! They fit because I created them. For fun. For pleasure. To be able to play on a field of dreams with no end in sight.

So, as you read my stories, dear reader, keep in mind that the Tesla car in my story is not Elon Musk's electric car, but a vehicle invented by collaboration between Thomas Edison and Nicolas Tesla in my invented world. It runs not by electricity as we know it, but by different energy discovered by Tesla.

In my world, Sherlock Holmes is not the first one of the stories, but one of several. Watson, likewise. Just as Spock was duplicated in the Star Trek series of movies to continue their worthy stories, so have I decided to include devices that will stimulate our imagination, take us to places we could never have gone before, and allow me to interject from time to time some of the wonderful insights I have been honored to receive as a maturing adult. So, death exists in my creation, but it has many permutations and outcomes. All exciting and mysterious.

Following this is a description of major characters, as well as items used exclusively in my Baker Street adventures.

Glossary of the Baker Street Universe

A list of players, places, and things that take place in the Baker Street Universe created by this author as the playground for his fantasies...and hopefully your own as well.

Bollocks...A common word used by the British to indicate something was nonsense, trash. An expletive.

Blaggart...a disagreeable person.

Drat, dratted...A swear word like damn to indicate frustration.

Pahalgam...A region of India at the foot of the Himalayas, next to the river Ganges. Very small village.

Ragmuffins...Homeless children that help Holmes out and whom he supports to keep off the streets.

Tosh...Sheer nonsense and an unkind reference to the upper class at that time.

Tesla Car...The device built by Ford in collaboration with Nicolas Tesla. Powered by a new form of energy unknown to our world yet.

Tesla devices...created by the team of Henry Ford, Thomas Edison, and Nicolas Tesla. Anything from lamps to frigs, to cooking devices. You name it; they've probably invented it in my world.

Moriarity...one of many. Professor Moriarity lives on in many and various manifestations for the sake of conflict, as well as invention and discourse. Where would a great detective be without a great villain to oppose him? While I don't feature Moriarity all the time, be warned he lurks behind the scenes! A lot!

Sherlock Holmes...A young man in his early twenties comes from a humble home and a good upbringing. Precocious with a perfect memory. Not the cold fish of the Doyle series. Much kinder and humorous. Still with many of the same characteristics, but softened with a gentler personality, without losing the edges that give him an engaging purpose and deductions that are utterly amazing at times.

Watson, Doctor John... the hero of the China Wars. Lost first love in China. Now in love with Mrs. Hudson. Loves Holmes like a brother. Doctor. Never without his black bag in which he carries his medical supplies and forensics tools that he and Sherlock often use in their investigations. Stocky with a bit of a stomach because of his love of scones, which I constantly use as a play of humor about the man.

Mrs. Hudson...not just a landlady anymore, but an integral part of the detective team...supplying support, as well as emotional and sometimes physical support. The glue that binds Watson and Holmes together. Again, in her twenties like Watson and Holmes. Lovely, but not beautiful, except in her beautiful spirit and kindly nature. Resourceful. Very shrewd and intelligent.

Lady Shareen... Lord Graystone's companion. A beautiful woman with a huge heart. She is responsible for helping women achieve social and financial equality. She also works to uplift the poor and homeless.

Professor Langston...the Invisible Man...a well-meaning doctor, who concocted a cocktail of chemicals that has forever altered his atomic structure such that he can turn invisible at will, though during emotional times of stress he can lose control of his visibility.

Inspector Bloodstone...a cantankerous policeman who has raving red hair, and a temper to match at times. Works with Holmes a lot but prefers to work on his own. Distrusts some of the intuitive moments of Holmes, but overall will go with what he reveals as Holmes is more often right than wrong in his deductions.

Constable Evans...the long-lost son of Inspector Bloodstone. Also red-haired, like his father, but with no temper and a great personality. Everyone likes him.

Queen Mary of Scots...has never existed. Instead, this one is a derivation of Mary, who was beheaded, and Victoria. Much more intelligent, progressive, but a leader in every sense of the word.

Magic...exists in this world of Sherlock as does science. Both are equally as relevant to the action and scenery of the stories.

Fairie...a land that exists in parallel to Sherlock's world and through which Lord Graystone (Lord of the Jungle) came through to become part of the Baker Street Brotherhood.

Fairie is richly endowed with magical creatures and monsters, Elves, fairies, and other fun things, as well as endless realms of green Amazon-like lands. Dragons. Which have played a part in several of my first stories and a few later ones.

Nicolas Tesla...a genius who has dedicated his life to upgrading the quality of life for everyone on the planet. Witty, charming, and dangerous.

Harry Houdini...swarthy, suave, into magic in every way...physical and the real thing.

Professor Challenger...very tall, built like a bear, flaming red beard and hair. Quick to temper, but a kind man with a great mind. An adventurer beyond measure.

Captain Nemo...a reformed pirate with a mind that grasps mechanics that rivals Henry Ford and Nicolas Tesla. Is famous for his extremely powerful weapon of the sea...the Nautilus.

Jules Verne...a genius when it comes to theories and fiction, blonde, extremely friendly, caring, and adventurous. Teams up often with H.G. Wells, a friend he grew up with. Designer of the Master of the World, which is another set of Victorian adventures he uses to fight an invasion from Mars.

H.G. Wells...a brilliant writer and navigator. Contributes to the flying device Master of the World and its ability to fly through space and time. Very British and a bit stuffy at times.

Alexander Dumas...a French friend of Jules in one of the worlds I've created for Jules to explore in unique adventures that do not include H.G. Wells. A huge man with a lust for adventure and fighting.

Henry Ford...still an arrogant man, but more willing to help others, and often teams up with Tesla to do projects. Not prominent yet in my stories but working on it.

Master of the World...a huge flying machine that resembles a cross between a dirigible and a submarine that travels utilizing String theory, with an engine that converts string energy into fuel that can thrust the ship between parallel worlds, as well as back and forth in time. Created by Jules Verne, but later improved by H.G. Wells after their battle with the Martians detailed in my prior series starting with Invaders.

Lord Graystone...my version of Tarzan, but instead of being raised by apes, he was raised by a bull dragon. Highly educated and a loyal supporter of Queen Mary of Scots and husband of Lady Shareen. Sponsors numerous charities for the poor and unwanted. Champion of Fairie.

Hyde...Doctor Jekyll performs an experiment on himself that separates the evil portion of him into a unique entity. This entity is pure evil and pure energy. It can possess anyone and once having done so, become that person. Cause them to do the unthinkable to achieve its evil plans.

Doctor Jekyll...a kind, young teacher who has made a horrible miscalculation and created an abomination of himself.... Hyde! A creature that is pure evil.

Dracula...not the Bran Stoker version, but my own. Misunderstood, not eternal, and drinking human blood when no other choice is possible.

Conan Doyle...the dead Sir Arthur Conan Doyle brought from our world to the alternate reality which he is reborn into, healthy and young once more. Also, an integral part of the great detective's team at times.

Baker Street Brotherhood...a team of operatives who, upon occasion, help Sherlock and Watson in their missions. Some of the more notable ones are Lord Graystone (Lord of the Jungle), Madame Curie, Dracula, Professor Langston (The Invisible Man), Professor Challenger (also a Conan Doyle character), Sir Arthur Conan Doyle himself (reborn from our world to the new one without losing awareness of himself), Lady Shareen (our equivalent of Indiana Jones), Jules Verne and H.G. Wells.

Monk...a spiritual leader and teacher, who has an ashram and school at the foot of the Himalayas in Pahalgam and is considered enlightened.

Also, the first and only teacher that Holmes felt truly affectionate for and close to.

There are many, many more, but these are the most frequently guested characters in my stories and novels.

Request for Review

If you found some pleasure in reading my work, please take the time to leave a review for it. Authors can thrive or die for the lack of reviews.

Thanking you in advance for your kindness.

John

Author's Note

If you want to keep abreast of the latest news, follow me on my author site: www.bakerstreetuniverses.com

Connect with me on Twitter: @johnpirillo

Friend me at my Facebook page: John Pirillo, Author[1].

Join my Baker Street Universe group to get things I don't usually share with others, and to hash over the universe I've created with me and fellow authors and readers. I'll be having incredibly special giveaways, advance copies, and autographed work as well as other surprises to my friends who join me there.

My artwork is available at: https://john-pirillo.pixels.com/

---

1.   https://www.facebook.com/john.pirillo.3.

OTHER BOOKS BY THE AUTHOR

SHERLOCK HOLMES, MAMMOTH FANTASY, MURDER AND MYSTERY TALES 21

SHERLOCK HOLMES, MAMMOTH FANTASY, MURDER AND MYSTERY TALES 22

SHERLOCK HOLMES, MAMMOTH FANTASY, MURDER AND MYSTERY TALES 23

SHERLOCK HOLMES, MAMMOTH FANTASY, MURDER AND MYSTERY TALES 24

SHERLOCK HOLMES, MAMMOTH FANTASY, MURDER AND MYSTERY TALES 25

SHERLOCK HOLMES, MAMMOTH FANTASY, MURDER AND MYSTERY TALES 26

SHERLOCK HOLMES, MAMMOTH FANTASY, MURDER, AND MYSTERY TALES 27

SHERLOCK HOLMES, MAMMOTH FANTASY, MURDER, AND MYSTERY TALES 28

SHERLOCK HOLMES, MOST PECULIAR

SHIFTERS+

SHIFTERS2+

DOUBLE HOLMES 2

ABNOMALIES

BAKER STREET WIZARD

BAKER STREET WIZARD 2

BAKER STREET WIZARD 3

DEEP SILENCE

DOUBLE HOLMES

DOUBLE HOLMES 2

DOUBLE HOLMES 3

DOUBLE HOLMES 4

DOUBLE HOLMES 5

DOUBLE HOLMES 6

DOUBLE HOLMES 7

DOUBLE HOLMES 8

DOUBLE HOLMES 9

DOUBLE HOLMES 10

DOUBLE HOLMES 11

DOUBLE HOLMES 12

DOUBLE HOLMES 13

DOUBLE HOLMES 14

DOUBLE HOLMES 15

FORBIDDEN WORLD

GEARS WORLD

GEARS WORLD 2

GEARS WORLD 3

GEARS WORLD 4

GEARS WORLD 5

GEARS WORLD 6

HALLOWEEN TREATS

JOURNEY INTO THE UNKNOWN

JOURNEY TO THE CENTER OF THE EARTH

JOURNEY

JOURNEY 2

JOURNEY 3

MONSTER HUNTER

ROCKET MAN TIME STREAMS 2

ROCKET MAN, PHOENIX

ROCKET MAN, THE SECRET WAR

ROCKET MAN, TIME STREAMS

ROCKETMAN, ARCH OF TIME

SECRET ADVENTURES OF JULES VERNE AND

ALEXANDER DUMAS, THE SEA DEMON
SECRET ADVENTURES OF JULES VERNE AND
ALEXANDER DUMAS, HOLLOW EARTH
SHERLOCK HOLMES, BAKER STREET WIZARD
SHERLOCK HOLMES, BAKER STREET WIZARD 2
SHERLOCK HOLMES, BAKER STREET WIZARD 3
SHERLOCK HOLMES, BAKER STREET WIZARD 4
SHERLOCK HOLMES, BAKER STREET WIZARD 5
SHERLOCK HOLMES, DEADLY MASTER
SHERLOCK HOLMES, HALLOWEEN VAMPIRE TALES
SHSERLOCK HOLMES, WEREWOLVE TALES
SHERLOCK HOLMES, HALLOWEEN MONSTERS
SHERLOCK HOLMES, HALLOWEEN MONSTERS 2
SHERLOCK HOLMES, LORD OF THE TREES
SHERLOCK HOLMES, THE BAKER STREET UNIVERSE
SHERLOCK HOLMES, URBAN FANTASY MYSTERIES
SHERLOCK HOLMES, URBAN FANTASY MYSTERIES 2
SHERLOCK HOLMES, URBAN FANTASY MYSTERIES 3
SHIFTER 1-4
THE CTHULHU INCIDENT 1-5

Don't miss out!

Visit the website below and you can sign up to receive emails whenever John Pirillo publishes a new book. There's no charge and no obligation.

https://books2read.com/r/B-A-EMSD-XFJQC

BOOKS 2 READ

Connecting independent readers to independent writers.

Did you love *Sherlock Holmes, The Ghost Wars, Book Two: The War of Magic*?
Then you should read *Sherlock Holmes, A Tale Less Told*[1] by John Pirillo!

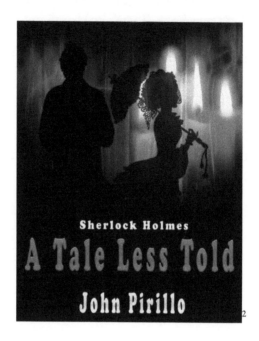

[2]

Sherlock Holmes has taken on unusual and dangerous cases.
   Cases that involve shapeshifters, vampires and werewolves...
   Dark, power-hungry wizards....
   But this time, it is different.
   It is personal.
   When Holmes returns home to 221B,
   he finds a mystery growing around his own friends.
   One by one they are mysteriously vanishing.
   Taken by an invisible force, which can strike unexpectedly.
   Holmes's loved ones are vanishing without a trace.
   Can Holmes save the ones he loves this time?
   Or is Christmas going to be desolate and empty for him?
   Read more at www.johnpirillo.com.

---

1. https://books2read.com/u/mBv05O

2. https://books2read.com/u/mBv05O

Also by John Pirillo

Angel Hamilton
Broken Fangs

Baker Street Universe Tales
Baker Street Universe Tales
Baker Street Universe Tales 2
Baker Street Universe Tales 3
Baker Street Universe Tales 4
Baker Street Universe Tales 5
Baker Street Universe Tales 6
Baker Street Universe Tales Seven

BAKER STREET WIZARD
Baker Street Wizard 4
Baker Street Wizard 5

Between
Prince of Between

"Classic Baker Street Universe Sherlock Holmes"
Sherlock Holme: Hyde's Night of Terror
Case of the Deadly Goddess
Case of the Abominable

Cythulhu
The Cthulhu Incident
The Eye of Cthulhu
The Throne of Cythulhu
Throne of Cthulhu
Giants of Cythulhu

Deadly
Sherlock Holmes, Deadly Master
Sherlock Holmes, Deadly Magic

Detective Judge Dee
Detective Dee Murder Most Chaste

Double Holmes
Sherlock Holmes, Double Holmes 2
Double Holmes 7
Double Holmes 8
Double Holmes 9
Double Holmes 10
Double Holmes 11
Double Holmes 12

Double Holmes 13
Double Holmes 14
Double Holmes 15
Double Holmes 16

Elektron
Elektron

Escape To Adventure
Escape to Adventure
Escape to Atlantis

FRACTAL UNIVERSE
Twist
Portal

G1, The Bureau of Extraordinary Investigations
Shifter 2+
Shifter 3+

Gears World
Gears World 5

Halloween
Sherlock Holmes, Halloween Monsters 2

Halloween Treats
Sherlock Holmes, Halloween Vampire Tales
Sherlock Holmes, Halloween Werewolf Tales

Hollow Earth Special Forces
Hollow Earth Special Forces, Forbidden World
Operation Deep Thrust
The Ancients

Holmes
Sherlock Holmes Struck
Sherlock Holmes A Dangerous Act

Infinite Tales
Infinite Tales 3
Infinite Tales 4
Infinite Tales 5
Infinite Tales 6
Infinite Tales 7
Infinite 8
Infinite Tales 9
Infinite Tales
Infinite Tales Two

Monster Hunter
Monster Hunter

Mystery Knight
HellBound Mystery
Hell Bound Angel

PhaseShift
PhaseShift
PhaseShift Two: Crossover
PhaseShift: Shifting Worlds

Rocketman
Rocketman
Rocket Man, Time Streams
Rocketman Christmas
Time Wars
Arch of Time

Secret Adventures of Jules Verne and Alexander Dumas
Hollow Earth
Hollow Earth

Sherlock Holmes
Sherlock Holmes, ICE
The Ice Man
Sherlock Holmes Fallen
Sherlock Holmes: Monster
Sherlock Holmes: Tick Tock
Sherlock Holmes Christmas Magic

Sherlock Holmes Dark Secret
Sherlock Holmes Shadow of Dorian Gray
Sherlock Holmes Vampire
Sherlock Holmes: Cursed in Stone
Sherlock Holmes Apparition
Sherlock Holmes Case of the Raging Madness
Sherlock Holmes Dark Princess
Sherlock Holmes Dark Angel
Constable Evans' Fancy
Sherlock Holmes Matter of Perception
Sherlock Holmes Tangled
Sherlock Holmes Case of the Gossamer Lady
Sherlock Holmes House of Shadows
Sherlock Holmes The Yellow Death
Sherlock Holmes Oblique
Sherlock Holmes Mystery Train Winter Collection
Sherlock Holmes A Tale Less Told
Sherlock Holmes Mystery Six
Sherlock Holmes, Rules of Darkness, Special Edition
Sherlock Holmes Shape of Justice
Sherlock Holmes Christmas Magic
Sherlock Holmes Fallen Angel
Ghostly Shadows
Sherlock Holmes Bloody Hell
Sherlock Holmes Monster of the Tower
Sherlock Holmes Darkest of Nights
Sherlock Holmes Nightmare
Sherlock Holmes Poetry of Death
Sherlock Holmes, Dracula
Sherlock Holmes #3, Ice Storm
Sherlock Holmes, Baker Street Wizard 3

Sherlock Holmes Double Holmes
Sherlock Holmes, Double Holmes 1

Sherlock Holmes, Mammoth Fantasy, Murder and Mystery Tales
Sherlock Holmes, Mammoth Fantasy, Murder, and Mystery Tales 15
Sherlock Holmes Mammoth Fantasy, Murder, and Mystery Tales 17
Sherlock Holmes Mammoth Fantasy, Murder, and Mystery Tales 26
Sherlock Holmes Mammoth Fantasy, Murder, and Mystery Tales 14

Sherlock Holmes, Mammoth Fantasy, Murder, and Mystery Tales 15
Sherlock, Holmes, Mammoth Fantasy, Murder, and Mystery Tales 15

Sherlock Holmes Urban Fantasy Mysteries
Sherlock Holmes Urban Fantasy Mysteries
Sherlock Holmes, Halloween Monsters
Sherlock Holmes Urban Fantasy Mysteries 2
Sherlock Holmes Urban Fantasy Mysteries 3
Sherlock Holmes, Urban Fantasy Mysteries 3
Sherlock Holmes Urban Fantasy Mysteries 4
Sherlock Holmes, Artifact
Sherlock Holmes, The Dracula Files
Sherlock Holmes, Dark Clues
Sherlock Holmes, Case of the Undying Man
Sherlock Holmes, Mystery of the Sea
Sherlock Holmes, Night Watch
Sherlock Holmes, Mystery of the Path not Taken
Sherlock Holmes, the Dorian Gray Affair
The Baker Street Universe
Sherlock Holmes, The Dracula Affair
Spector
Sherlock Holmes, Rules of Darkness
Sherlock Holmes, A Tale Less Told
Sherlock Holmes, The Christmas Star

Sherlock Holmes, Christmas Tales
Steampunk Holmes
Sherlock HOlmes, Deadly Valentine's Day
Sherlock Holmes, Angel Murders
Sherlock Holmes, Deadly Intent
Sherlock Holmes, White Diamond Mystery
Sherlock Holmes, Gears World, Box Set One
Sherlock Holmes, The Blue Fire of Harry Houdini
Sherlock Holmes, White Diamond Vampire Mystery
Sherlock Holmes, Black Tower
Sherlock Holmes, Tales of the Macabre
Sherlock Holmes, Baker Street Wizard
Sherlock Holmes, Usher
Sherlock Holmes, Baker Street Wizard 2
Sherlock Holmes, Double Holmes 1
Sherlock Holmes, Cave of the Dark Elf
Sherlock Holmes, Something Wicked
Sherlock Holmes, Gears Word 3
Sherlock Holmes, Gears World 4
Sherlock Holmes, Deadly
Sherlock Holmes, Urban Fantasy Mysteries Six
Werewolves
Sherlock Holmes, Mammoth Fantasy, Murder, and Mystery Tales 27
Sherlock Holmes, Urban Fantasy Mysteries
Sherlock Holmes, Lord of the Trees
Sherlock Holmes, The Ghost Wars, Book One, Rise of the Ghost Empire

Sherlock Holmes, Urban Fantasy Mystery Tales
Sherlock Holmes, Urban Fantasy Mystery Tales 2
Sherlock Holmes, Dark Matters
Sherlock Holmes, Black Wizard
Sherlock Holmes, Curse of the Black Wizard
Sherlock Holmes, The Ghost Wars, Book Two: The War of Magic

Sky Captain Adventures
Sky Captain Adventures 2, Zombie World
SKY CAPTAIN ADVENTURES 3

Steampunk Holmes
Sherlock Holmes, Gears of the Goddess

The Baker Street Detective
The Baker Street Detective 5, The Howling Wind
Strange Times, The Baker Street Detective, Book2
The Baker Street Detective, Hollow Man
Sherlock Holmes, Baker Street Detectives

Thrilling Mystery Tales
Thrilling Mystery Tales 2

Twist
Twist 2
Twister

Urban Fantasies
Urban Fantasies 1
Urban Fantasies 3
Urban Fantasies

War of the Worlds
Battle for Earth

WireShip
Wirestation Red Lion

Standalone
Sherlock Holmes Deadly Consequences
Invisibility Factor
Red Painted Souls
Between
Robin Hood
Shadow Man
The Rainbow Bridge
Cartoon, Johnnie Angel
Sherlock Holmes 221B
Sherlock Holmes Shape Shifter
Urban Fantasy Mysteries
Sherlock Holmes, Urban Fantasy Mysteries
Halloween Mysteries
Invasion
Romancing the Word
Romancing the Word Workbook
Sherlock Holmes, Gears World 2
Thrilling Mystery Tales
Weird Short Tales
Spectre Forces
Young King Arthur
Dark Midnight
Anomalies

Shifter+
Shifter 4+
Deep Silence
Sherlock Holmes, Halloween Fantasies
Sherlock Holmes, Halloween Terror
Sherlock Holmes, Halloween Terror 2

Watch for more at www.johnpirillo.com.

Milton Keynes UK
Ingram Content Group UK Ltd.
UKHW010308301123
433483UK00002B/182